THE
BLOOD
ON MY
HANDS..

Also by Gaurav Dashputra

And then it rained....

THE
BLOOD
ON MY
HANDS..

Gaurav Dashputra ● Siddhant Kaushik

Srishti
PUBLISHERS & DISTRIBUTORS

SRISHTI PUBLISHERS & DISTRIBUTORS
N-16, C. R. Park
New Delhi 110 019
editorial@srishtipublishers.com

First published by
Srishti Publishers & Distributors in 2014

Typeset by Eshu Graphic

This is a story about the mystical journey called life
and its only destination: *death*.

"What hands are here? Ha! They pluck out mine eyes!
Will all great Neptune's oceans wash this blood
Clean from my hand? No; this my hand will rather
The multitudinous seas incarnadine,
Making the green one, red!"

— *Macbeth*, Shakespeare.

ACKNOWLEDGEMENTS

We extend heartfelt thanks to our parents for all the support they have given us and for coping with us during our night-long phone calls and creative sessions, that we so frequently got involved in.

We would like to thank our immediate and extended family for their encouragement.

A sincere thanks to all our friends for their enthusiasm towards our venture and it is an absolute pleasure to have you guys by our side.

A big thank you to all our friends and followers on social networking sites, i.e. Facebook, Twitter, Quora, etc. Your undying love for us is something we take a lot of pride in.

We would also like to show gratitude to all the readers of And Then It Rained.... It is because of your love and support that we could garner the courage of venturing into these eddy waters again; metaphorically ;)

We are extremely grateful to Mr. Rahul Puri for taking time out of his extremely busy schedule and writing a heart-warming foreword for us. Thanks a lot sir for your kind words and support.

We have an enormous sense of gratitude towards Whistling Woods International and all the faculty members for their support in our venture and helping us with this book. A special thanks to Mr. Anjum Rajabali and Mr. Prabodh Parikh for sharpening our skills of storytelling through your most valuable lectures.

We would like to thank the publishers for their unwavering faith in us and forming a formidable author-publisher relationship.

Last but not the least, we would like to thank Mr. Sunill Kaushik and InkStudioz for designing a fantastic cover page.

FOREWORD

It's always nice to be asked to write the foreword of a book. Nicer when the book is written by one of your students. I have always been a fan of spy thrillers but when Gaurav asked me to write the foreword to his book, I honestly was unsure of whether I should or not. I don't really know if I am qualified to write a foreword of a book. Yes, as mentioned, am a huge fan of the genre but am not a screenwriter or a novelist. Then I decided to read the material he sent and I started to believe that this book was right down my alley. The kind of book, film, content that I love and thrive on. I was quickly motivated to read more and more and when I finished, I was suddenly comfortable writing a foreword, a review, anything to help Gaurav and the book.

The Blood on My Hands is an electric read. The story pulsates from first page to last and in Rehan Irani, the author has written a character with so many interesting shades that, despite his profession, he is instantly relatable. I hope that I get to read more of Rehan because clearly this story should not be the last of him. Set in a world based on cold hard reality, the novel talks about love and retribution, but mixes it with action and drama, making for a story which has pace as well as a heart. Something that is rare. Gaurav has shown a lot of promise with this novel, which is his second to be published. I believe this is the first in series in which he intends to expand on the characters and I hope he does. Besides being a talented writer, he is also studying to be a filmmaker and I have no doubt that this experience will make his writing even more engaging and expressive. He already brings with him such an interesting range of experiences from studying medicine to now working on being a cinematographer. I wish him the very best and hope that he continues to write and churn out terrific novels like *The Blood on My Hands*.

— Rahul Puri

PROLOGUE

The slick road glistened under the headlights as a lone truck rumbled slowly to a stop in the middle of nowhere on the Old Goa Highway; the suspension almost weighed to its limits by the scrap iron that bulged out the sides of the carrier. A small figure got down on the passenger side, stepping gingerly as if the long haul had stiffened his muscles. Raindrops shone like gold as the figure crossed towards the driver's side illuminated by the yellow wash revealing a boy, about five feet tall, wearing a black wind cheater, shorts and carrying a backpack. He looked like a typical school going kid, that is, until you noticed his lopsided silhouette and grim expression. One of his sleeves flapped aimlessly in the wind. His right arm had been amputated from the elbow and if not for the yellow light giving it color, his face would have appeared lifeless.

'Thank you for the lift,' he told the truck driver.

'You sure you want to get down here boy? There isn't anything around for miles. I can still drop you at the next village,' the driver said. His conscience bit him for leaving a lad so young in the middle of a desolate highway. But the boy had paid him five grand to soothe the ache. The boy had approached him at one of his pit stops in the city with the proposition along with the sweetener for anonymity. He could live with it if it came down to that, no questions asked.

'No, no, I am fine. My friends will be here any minute to pick me up,' the boy said.

Why would anyone set this as a pick up spot? the driver thought. 'Are you sure you don't want me to stay till then?' he asked the boy.

'Yes, I am sure. Thanks again,' the boy said.

'Okay then.' The driver turned on the ignition and drove off.

The boy stood on the edge of the highway watching the truck as its red tail blazed a path through the rain vanishing in the distance. He looked both ways to make sure that the highway was deserted and realized the futility of such an action. It was, after all, almost 3 a.m. on a rainy night, miles away from the nearest village. Convinced that there wasn't anyone watching him, he turned and started walking towards the woods that darkened the already grey landscape to the side of the highway. After about fifty metres he could see the blackness looming in front of him, so he put his backpack on the ground and opened it using his only hand. A pre-disposed righty, but the years had taught him well to use what he was left with. He removed a flashlight from the backpack and positioned it below his chin as he tried to zip the backpack shut. The flashlight slipped and fell down on the ground, which made it break open.

Shit...Shit...Shit. I hate living like this. Slinging the backpack around his stump, he picked up the flashlight and placed it in his mouth. He then picked up the batteries and inserted them in the flashlight, still holding it in his mouth. His thoughts wandered towards the self-pitying *'if only I had my hand'* but he had walled himself against such fancies a long time ago and his resolution made him press on.

The boy switched the flashlight on, giving vivid detail to the inky blackness that was. Withered leaves lay scattered all over and the raindrops made a rattling noise as they fell on them while he trudged on crunching through the foliage. Turning around, he could not see the highway now. A slight sense of fear overtook him but he continued further into the woods.

He saw a small cliff in front of him on which stood a huge banyan tree, almost as old as the boulders surrounding it. He headed towards it, snaking a path through the thorny shrubbery, his breath getting shallower and faster with every step he took. The cliff turned out to be steeper than he had expected but somehow he managed to crawl to the top. Standing under the tree, he pointed the flashlight at it, as if studying its form. Shaking his head, he walked in a circle around the trunk, all the while observing carefully, brushing away the limp roots that hung all around.

This is it. He put the flashlight back into his backpack and stood at the edge of the cliff. He could see city lights shining dimly far away. He closed his eyes and placed the palm of his hand on his chest and mumbled something under his breath. Perhaps, muttered a prayer.

He then turned around and started climbing the tree. It was a fairly effortless climb for him considering he had just one arm. It seemed as if he had practiced it. Soon he was sitting on a branch pretty high up. Balancing carefully, he opened his backpack and pulled out a coil of rope which he slowly let slither to the ground holding one end tight. He tied this loose end to the branch and looked down.

About fifteen feet. He then pulled the rope up revealing that the other end had already been fashioned into a noose with the help of a slipknot. He slowly raised the noose with his hand and stared at it. The rain was masking the sweat that was trickling down his forehead.

He stood up carefully on the branch and saw lightning strike somewhere in the city far away. The sudden flash bringing the whole landscape into sharp relief. It was a gorgeous view and he wanted to take it all in. '*Don't do it. This is not the way.*' A voice echoed in his head. He closed his eyes and took three deep breaths. He then picked up the noose and pulled it over his head and around his neck.

'There is no other way. This is the only way.' He said, as if in meek submission to his own weakness and jumped off the branch.

A loud thud accompanied by a groan was heard as he smashed into the ground. The boy lay there motionless for a second.

'Fuck! Shit! Fuck Shit!' He knew his rope had turned out to be too long and now he could not move.

His pain was intense and he was writhing on the ground. The sound of his cries echoed through the woods. This wasn't the fate he had chosen for himself. This wasn't the death he wanted to die. But then, when had life given him what he wanted? His sad demise was to be a testament to his depressed life; and that somehow made him smile as he drifted into the same blackness as was around him.

❚❚❚

Awakened by the ghoulish dream, Rehan found himself sitting up on his bed. Beads of sweat dribbled down his forehead slowly; his heart was thumping speedily in his chest and his breathing rapid. The rays of the sun crept inside the room through a gap in the curtains creating a Tyndall effect. Dreams had a way of freaking Rehan out. He thought that these freaky dreams came with his job but the details...the details and the elaborate way in which he pictured and remembered them distressed him. He longed for that one night when he would sleep and have no dreams.

Rehan looked at the woman lying down next to him. Even in her sleep she looked serene and completely beautiful. If given a choice, all he would do was lie down next to her and watch her sleep or talk or eat...he would just look at her and look after her. But it was already 8 a.m. and he had to go. The funeral was today. Even though he did not feel like going because he had no idea what he was going to say, but he had to go. That was the right thing to do. All his life he had made bad choices and wrong calls, but now he was going to change it all. From now on, he was going to do things his way...the right way. And with that thought, he got up and walked to the bathroom to get ready for the funeral.

PART

I

A JOB UNDONE

7th June 2013
Bandra, Mumbai

The colonial bungalow on Carter Road seemed completely out of place when one compared it to the modern paper-like buildings surrounding it. The brick brown paint on the outer walls to mask the strong stone walls underneath, the spacious manicured lawn, the shiny vintage Jaguar resting in the shade usually traversing a cobbled path that led to a huge wooden gate outside made the whole feel of the house very Victorian.

The residents of the house took great pride in calling it their home as was evident from that bold nameplate placed right next to the security guard's station.

"THE PURIS" the plate shouted out. Everyone in Bandra knew about the Puri house but if you asked them what they did or how they looked, no one could give you an accurate answer. As proprietors of such a majestic property, the Puris were a reserved lot. They never hosted any grand parties, nor did they have many guests over.

If not for the slight breeze making things pleasant, this typical drizzly Mumbai monsoon evening would have taken a turn towards the unpleasant. Taking advantage of this beautiful weather was Missus Puri, cloistered in her house, watching television in the living room on a huge plasma screen that adorned most part of the wall. Around her, the interiors looked both pricey and modern, a slight difference how the house appeared from the outside. A huge red velvet couch was placed right in the middle of the room facing the big screen in front of which was a large centre table made of glass with a convoluted piece of polished wood serving as its stand. A crystal chandelier hung down from the ceiling and plush carpets covered the floor. A narrow hallway, rarely used except by the man who owned it all, studded with doors leading to different parts of the house decked by some potted plants, led to the stairs at the far end of the house which went up to the study.

Colonel Puri usually spent most of his time sitting in the study on a large leather armchair in front of the fireplace smoking his pipe, sometimes reading, sometimes looking at the paintings adorning his walls as if trying to relive what they showed. Unlike Missus Puri, the Colonel's taste in interiors was antique, yet exquisite. So three years ago, when they had moved in to this splendid house, he had taken it upon himself to oversee the designing of the study. A Caucasian rug was spread over the entire floor. The walls were turned into tall bookshelves that housed over a thousand books. Fancy corbels decorated the ceiling. A study table made of hard maple wood, three revolving chairs placed around it and a leather armchair next to the fireplace was all the furniture that was there in the room. A huge portrait of a young boy sitting on a sculpted wooden chair with stylized surroundings was placed on the wall over the fireplace, which in contrast to the whole room seemed quite plain.

Colonel Puri stared at the portrait absently. For a man who was forty-five years old, he looked much older. The lines etched on his face told the tale of a hard and horrid past while his shrewd and thoughtful eyes, besides the obvious lavishness of his surroundings, showed his ability to overcome all that life could throw at him. The balding head and the grey hair weren't genetic, but more of a bodily response to prolonged periods of stress and emotional distress. But all that was now a thing of the past. He knew that. It had taken all his will and might to reach where he was now. Three years ago he had taken voluntary retirement from the Army and turned his life around for his own good. He now lived his life the way he wanted to and there wasn't a goddamn thing anyone could do about it. But he would have liked to see them try.

Still looking at the portrait, he took another puff from his pipe and exhaled a cloud of swirling white smoke that left just a hint of lavender in the air. He then looked down at the fire that illuminated his face.

Why the hell do I need a fireplace in Mumbai? What was I thinking? he thought. The thought managed to bring a rare smile to his face. He then turned his attention back to the portrait and gazed at it inattentively. He knew all the details and yet looking at it made him re-visit the past and strengthen the resolve that made him live his life now. The light touch of a smaller hand in his, the last walk in a forest, and the tears in his eyes as cold metal turned warm against his palms almost crushing him with its weight.

The ringing of his cell phone made him blink. His expressions showing evident agitation directed towards the timing of the phone call. Anyone who knew him was well aware that he did not like being disturbed when he was in the study. Vexed, he picked up the phone.

'Hello,' he said in the curt voice that still hinted at his military bearing.

'Hi, is this The Greener Pastures Company?' said the man on the other side of the line.

'Yes,' replied Colonel Puri.

'Good, I have a pasture that needs some greening,' the voice chuckled.

'Do we already have a contract?' Colonel asked.

'We don't,' said the man.

'Then I am sorry sir. I can't accept the assignment right now. You can come down to our office tomorrow and we will go over the contract and the other formalities,' the Colonel said calmly.

'I am afraid there is no time for that. This is...how should I say...an emergency,' said the man. 'I am sure you can make some kind of arrangement at such short notice.'

'What is the client's name?'

'Mr. T.V. Fernandez,' said the man.

The Colonel scratched his brow and thought for a bit. Ever since he had started The Greener Pastures Company a couple of years ago, he had accepted plenty of assignments on emergency basis but he wasn't a big fan of theirs. He was a pre-meditative guy and any deviations didn't go down well with him. Besides, an urgent request always made him doubt its genuineness and that made him a little nervous.

'How do I know that is a proper assignment and not counterfeit?' Colonel Puri asked.

A brief giggling noise came from the other side of the line. 'Don't worry; this call is not a fake. I know about your payment policy and I am wiring the money to your account mentioned on the secret forum as we speak. A mail regarding the details of the assignment and the client has also been sent to you. The details are in every sixth line of the content as requested in the forum. After confirming the transfer, I don't think you will doubt me,' the man said.

'Will you just hold on for a minute, sir?' The Colonel said.

'Sure.'

Colonel Puri got up from his armchair and made his way towards the study table. He placed his cell phone down on the table and sat down on the revolving chair behind it. He pulled open the drawer and took out his laptop. He drew up the screen and it came to life instantly. He leaned forward towards the screen and placed his finger on the track pad. Carefully moving the cursor over the web browser's icon, the Colonel clicked on it. The log in page of Citibank popped open. He typed in his username and password. His eyes immediately went to the top right corner of the screen where the option of Recent Activity was. He selected it. It said –

7th June 2013:21:15 hours – Your account XXXXXXXXXX0912 has been credited with 1,00,00,000 INR.

Colonel picked up the phone. 'The assignment has been accepted. Don't worry, everything will be arranged tonight itself.'

'Very well then,' said the man and hung up.

Colonel Puri then opened his mail account. He had a new mail with the subject – Assignment Details. He opened it and wrote down every sixth line on a piece of paper. The looping cursive was quite contrary to his stern personality; the page read

Client Name – Mr. T.V. Fernandez.

Location – Sterling CHS, Flat 501, J.P Road, Seven Bungalow Garden, Versova, Mumbai.

Deleting the mail, he then picked up his phone and placed a call.

'Hello Rehan, Colonel this side. We have a new assignment for tonight. Arif will have all the details. Get in touch with him and take care of it tonight,' he said and took a deep breath. 'And listen…be careful.'

The Colonel disconnected the line and quickly sent a text message to Arif asking him to meet him in his study right away. He then opened a cabinet lined with glass bottles. He took out a bottle labeled *Teacher's 50* and a crystal glass. After pouring himself a round of whiskey, he placed the bottle on the table itself and headed back towards the fireplace. He sat down on the armchair and took a sip from the glass. The whiskey made him feel a little more relaxed and allowed him to drift through time.

About half an hour later, someone knocked at the door.

'Come in,' he said.

In walked a man who looked to be in his early thirties and went straight to the Colonel.

'A drink?' asked the Colonel.

The man knew it was a test and shook his head. The Colonel smiled as he passed him the piece of paper.

'Memorize this. Rehan will be in touch with you shortly. It'll have to be tonight.'

Arif looked at the paper for a second and without giving it further thought, he crumpled it and tossed it into the fire in front of him.

'It'll be done boss,' he smiled. But it wasn't a wicked one. It looked as if all he aimed for was to please the Colonel.

'I knew my sister had made the right choice when I saw you.' He paused, and then said, 'Give him a clean death.'

Arif nodded, turned and left the room closing the door softly behind him.

Colonel Puri took another swig at his drink and rested his glance back on the portrait. The rain continued to pour outside.

It was one of those rare nights in Mumbai when the city of eternal lights was covered in darkness. Blackouts weren't a common occurring in the Maximum City and when they did occur, one could be sure that it was because of some technical problems and not to be sorted out very soon. Patience was a virtue overly tested here. Over the past couple of hours, the rain had acquired more intensity, which in turn had led to a short circuit at the electricity board. A few lucky people with back up inverters at home were the only ones who had lights turned on in their houses but they too would soon run out if this continued. The roads, always lit by headlights and full of people failing their everyday tests, honking with impatience, seemed liked the bustling veins of a sleeping giant. But apart from that the city only winked when streaks of lightening flashed across the sky.

All the buildings looked almost identical in the swarthiness of Mumbai. One would think that the day might add significant differentiable details but one would be disappointed. Just identical squares piled on top of each other.

A pair of headlights glided over JP Road. They went out abruptly as the car pulled over outside Sterling Co-operative

Housing Society. It was a black Chevrolet sedan with tinted windows. All that could be seen were the shadows of the two men inside. A couple of minutes later the doors flew open and the men got down from the car. They both carried black umbrellas in gloved hands as they walked through the rain towards the gate of Sterling Society. They halted briefly at the gate and looked at the guard's station before moving along. The security guard had been sound asleep and they saw no point in bothering him. They walked into the building and laid down their umbrellas on the floor.

'Gosh! We will have to climb up five floors.' Arif said.

'Wow! Aren't you the genius?' Rehan mocked Arif sarcastically.

'There is no denying that,' said Arif as he wiped off the drops of water on his coat with his hand. 'I don't think I have the stamina to climb five floors man. Why don't you go upstairs alone? I will stay here.'

'And what makes you think I have the stamina. I am no better than you,' Rehan said knowing at the back of his mind that he probably was. But he wasn't falling for the same old 'gosh I am too lazy to do my own goddamn job' crap all over again. Also, one always needed backup in his line of work considering the occupational hazards.

'That is also true. We both are chimneys man. It's high time we stopped smoking so much.'

'Amen to that brother.' *As if that was gonna happen. God, as usual, won't be straining his ears for this one.* 'Now let's go finish this off,' Rehan said and they made their way up the stairs.

Two yellow circles illuminated the dank landing on the fifth floor as they walked silently to the first door made of polished wood with gold lettering. Standing on either side of the door,

Arif peeked through the keyhole, while Rehan tried to hear any sound that might be coming from inside. Nothing.

'Just a candle,' Arif whispered.

Satisfied, he tried the handle and the door clicked open. They exchanged a look of surprise and apprehension.

▌▌▌

Apartment 501 was one of those typical two bedroom, hall, kitchen apartments which were pretty plebeian to Mumbai. There was a small wooden coffee table placed in the centre of the living room on which a single candle flickered, illuminating the otherwise dark room. A few pills in a bowl and a pack of cigarettes also lay on the coffee table. The interiors of the living room were drab and highly suggestive of geriatric inhabitancy.

Tony Vivian Fernandez was a man in his late fifties. He sat on a rocking chair in the living room of the apartment wearing pyjamas and puffing on his cigarette. His brown eyes were looking intently at the grandfather clock that stood against the wall next to the doorway. His face looked as if someone had sucked the life out of it, pale and gaunt. Usually a man his age would be potbellied but he was abnormally undernourished and his body resembled that of a thirteen-year-old with marasmus. It had been over a week now that he had been living on just smoke, pills and water. The rubbish in the kitchen reeked slightly. A thin layer of dust on the furniture showed its level of disuse.

The grandfather clock showed the time as 1:18 a.m. as it ticked regularly. With every ticking sound, the clock made Fernandez grow more and more queasy. His anxiety was evident from his profuse sweating. He took another slow long drag from his cigarette as the clock struck 1:19 a.m.

Time is such a funny concept, Fernandez thought as he sighed and wiped the beads of sweat from his forehead, not taking his gaze off the clock. The thoughts were still flowing in his head. *'Time is such a funny concept, yet it is what people model their lives around. It is an organizational tool, a way of measuring the instants of the moments that remain. The final destination for our time is unknown…usually. But when it is known, time seems to be the longest lasting real thing on this planet and also the shortest.'* He had always enjoyed paradoxes, but now, living in one inspired fear.

He took another puff at his cigarette as the clock changed to 1:20 a.m. In between the battering of the rain outside, the ticking of the clock and the crackling of his burning cigarette, Fernandez heard a click. He heard the front door creak as it opened and was gently closed, the shuffling footsteps as two men emerged from the doorway. One of them had a ponytail and a small goatee. He was shorter than the other who had his hair spiked up. Fernandez looked up at them, his eyes wide in the gleam of the candle with a look of fear and a hint of something else that Rehan found eerie in such a place…hope. They were both wearing black suits and white shirts. The taller one was wearing a simple narrow black tie while the shorter guy wore a red one. They stared at him coldly. Fernandez opened his mouth and was about to speak when two simultaneous silenced gunshots were fired. The chair rocked vigorously from the recoil of his body. Fernandez had been shot in the head twice. His body then slowly slid off the rocking chair, leaving behind a trail of blood.

Rehan removed his sunglasses and looked down at the dead man as he lowered his silver Silenced AMT Hardballer pistol. Arif sheathed his .45 ACP Colt M1911 inside his coat pocket and leaned down to inspect the body. He took out a cell phone from the pockets of Fernandez' pyjamas and instantly dismantled it. Arif then removed the SIM card, dropped the phone on the floor and stomped on it thrice.

'Search for the laptop, will you?' he told Rehan.

Rehan looked around the room briefly and spotted the laptop kept on the dinner table outside the kitchen. 'Found it.'

'Good,' Arif said as he picked up the lighter from the coffee table and set the SIM card on fire. He then pulled out a cigarette and lit it up from the flaming SIM card before tossing it into the trashcan.

'I thought you were going to quit,' Rehan said.

'Man, this job stresses me out, so stop taking my case, will you?'

'Sure.' Rehan smirked, 'So what should we do with the laptop?'

'Let's take it back to Satan. He will know how to dispose it off.'

'Hey what is with you calling the Colonel, Satan? I know it suits him very well but he is your wife's brother. Why do you despise him so much?' Rehan inquired.

'I don't despise him, man. I am fucking scared of him. And you know that Arif Mohammad ain't scared of nobody.'

'Yep, and I also know that Arif Mohammad is a wannabe rapper born in a completely wrong country.' Rehan said as he took the cigarette from Arif and took a drag from it.

'Hip Hop is my passion man, just like kung fu and trumpets are your love. So who cares if I was born in Lucknow or Los Angeles?' Arif said snatching the cigarette back.

'Firstly, it is taekwondo and saxophone. And secondly, look at you, you came to Mumbai to become a rapper and what have you turned into; a hitman.'

Arif did not pay much attention to Rehan's words and walked away into the bedroom of the apartment. 'Do you think there's anything worth taking in here?' He asked.

'Maybe, there might be.'

Protocol dictated that the scene should look like a theft that got out of hand and resulted in murder. The police already overloaded with such cases rarely looked twice. Arif had a different philosophy altogether. He said that if one was making it look like a theft, one might as well steal some. It made sense in a way.

Rehan glanced into the bedroom and saw Arif tearing through the stuff and searching for valuables, which might have been locked away. He then entered the kitchen and abruptly stopped. There was a fridge in the kitchen, the surface of which was almost entirely covered with pictures. Rehan pulled the flashlight out of his coat pocket and turned it on. He focused it on a particular picture and stared at it intensely.

'Hey Arif, come over here,' he called out.

Arif came over from the bedroom holding a ring in his hand. 'What is it?'

'Have a look,' Rehan said.

Arif looked at the picture and his mouth dropped open. It was a picture of Mister Fernandez with a curly–haired girl clicked on a beach. There were numerous other solo pictures of the girl clicked at different places and at different times. Arif reached over and pulled one of the pictures off. He gazed at it for a few seconds and then turned to look at Rehan who was still staring at the pictures.

'Forget about it man.' Arif said. 'It was like what, twenty years ago?'

'Seven, actually.'

Arif crumpled the picture in his hand and threw it the garbage can. He walked away into the living room without giving Rehan a second glance. 'Screw it; let's get out of here. We'll go hit the bar or something,' he said.

Rehan nodded but continued to stare at the fridge. He then retrieved the picture from the garbage and slid it into his coat pocket. He couldn't just throw all those memories away. Arif was carrying the laptop and was pacing around the door making chairs topple. He let a vase crash to the floor and disheveled the rug. Rehan came out from the kitchen and saw the corpse of Fernandez lying down on the floor in his own pool of blood. He went and knelt next to it and ran his hand over his hair. A few drops of tears rolled down his eyes and over his cheeks.

CRASH... the coffee table was upended while the candle, still stuck, burned sideways with wax dropping to the floor.

Startled, he quickly wiped his tears off, extinguished the candle and made his way out of apartment 501 closing the door behind him.

8th June 2013
Colaba, Mumbai

The sky was slowly changing its colour, from black to grey and then a light blue. The chirping of the birds could be heard all around as they flew across the sky in their typical 'v' formations, possibly claiming victory over the skies. The melodic chant of the *fajr namaz,* the first prayer of the day could be heard loud and clear from the mosque in the distance. Cars had started whizzing by on relatively empty streets. The local trains and buses had commenced their services of commuting people around the city. In no time, Mumbai would return to its hustle bustle and the streets would be chock-a-block. The pace would have to be quickened if one still wanted to breathe oxygen.

Like most mornings, Rehan Irani was jogging on the pavement of Marine Drive. At the age of twenty-seven, his life was anything but normal. But apart from playing the saxophone and sharpening his martial art skills, this was one of those things that gave him immense pleasure. Seeing Mumbai come to life every morning right in front of him somehow made him bustle with the same energy. Life in this city was like one big cluster-fuck of myriad variables. Everyone was always on the move, trying to stay a step ahead of the others, collectively blocking the path for each other.

So many places to be...offices, jobs, schools, colleges; the tenants of a normal life that people all around him led. This always made Rehan feel distant from everyone else as if he were an observer, an outsider, but yet, a part of the city, much like an eagle circling up in the sky feels part of the forest but never one with it.

Rehan stopped jogging as he reached a street vendor who was selling tea and coffee out of two containers placed on a bicycle. These literal peddlers needed to be mobile ever since the ban on public smoking, but mornings were pretty peaceful. He ordered a coffee and sat down on a bench nearby. The streets grew more crowded with every passing minute and Rehan saw the passers-by while he sipped his coffee and puffed on a cigarette.

Rehan had always liked his role as an observer. He liked watching people but never seemed to participate; that was just not his thing. He liked to watch people and sometimes, just sometimes, he imagined what sort of a person they were, from their appearance and behaviour. He took another long sip of his coffee and dropped the cigarette to the ground. A lady speaking on a cell phone passed him by almost at a trot. She didn't even turn her head, but merely walked right past him in dark yoga pants, a fluorescent pink tank top, earphones plugged to an armband and streaked hair in a tight ponytail. One look at her and Rehan knew that she was the type who felt high up in this world. He knew that she didn't have time to look at others, and how could one who seemed so self-absorbed? She was the opposite of him, probably an owl. He then thought that he was being self absorbed by stereotyping her as an owl just because she didn't look at him. One of the reasons for observing people was that one got to understand so much about oneself.

As Rehan took another swig from his coffee, a fat man walked him by. He stopped right in the middle of the road and scratched his arse directly in front of Rehan while he bought a packet of Classic Milds and then continued walking. A smile crept up on Rehan's face. This was why he loved his early morning jogs. It made him forget about his miserable life, if only for a couple of hours. He finished his coffee and made his way towards the taxi stand on Nariman Point. The sun was now high and it would soon be hell outside.

'Colaba Causeway,' he told the cabbie.

▌▌▌

Rehan's apartment was located on the seventh floor of a building right opposite the street market of Causeway. It was a small threadbare studio apartment ready to crumble without a moment's notice. The walls were plain off white and unadorned and the layout showed no inclination of the tenant to make that house his home. It was not that he couldn't afford a better place, but he preferred it this way. It gave him the anonymity he needed to pursue his line of work and also the solitude to cope up with the after effects. Plus the place came with a balcony that overlooked the main road below. It gave him the eyrie befitting his role in the teeming forest that lay below. He liked spending time on the balcony as the people got involved with their drunken merrymaking. There was something so pure and honest about an inebriated man; something that he missed in himself now.

Rehan hadn't slept much all night. The whole episode of last night was still fresh in his head. He had been doing what he did for around two years now and never had an assignment troubled him so much. Every time he closed his eyes and tried to doze off, the picture of the girl would pop up right in front of his eyes. The girl, with her curly hair, the milky complexion and her hazel eyes; the memory so vivid as if it was just yesterday even though this huge swath of time separated him from his last glimpse of that perfect face. The first stone had rolled down the cliff and he didn't want to get caught up in the snowball effect. He could do little to offset his predicament though and this always left him buried under the landslide of his own emotions.

When Rehan had started working for Colonel Puri, it was this foresight that made him expect that he would suffer from a lot of sleepless nights and just for that he had purchased prescription based sleeping pills, but to his surprise, had never felt the need to consume them till today. He picked up the bottle of Diazepam and took out two pills. He then gulped them down with a glass of water and lay down on his couch. He turned the television on and started flipping through channels. Animal Planet was showing a shark special episode. Rehan let out an awkward laugh for no apparent reason. He felt the medication taking its effect on him. A shark attacked a seal and ripped it up as Rehan slept soundly.

❚❚❚

The unearthly blaring of horns woke Rehan up with just the reminiscence of a pair of haughty hazel eyes extremely disappointed in him. It was eight thirty in the evening and the fun and frolic had begun on Causeway, apparent by the merry chatter and incessant honking on the road below. He got up from the couch, went to the water closet and splashed some water on his face. After taking a leak he fetched a beer from his fridge and went out onto the balcony. He lit up a cigarette and took a sip from his beer as he stared over the balcony blankly, remembering the expression on Arif's face when he saw the pictures on the fridge. It had been one of those drunken one to one's that had made him blurt his story out, relieving the poison to make way for the one he was ingesting, even if only for the night.

A group of drunken teenagers stumbled along the sidewalk as they yelled obscene things at each other.

'*Get out of it*' Rehan reproached himself and sighed at the loneliness around him.

One needed distractions at times to cope up with all that life throws at you.

He saw a young man vomiting all over the sidewalk outside Leopold's Café. His friends howled with laughter. For the first time in his life, Rehan did not want to be the observer. He too wanted to go out with his friends and chill out somewhere. But friends had now become an alien concept for him, he had none and the closest thing he had to one was his damned partner. Rehan tossed his cigarette over the balcony and walked inside.

He pulled out a big black case from under the couch and opened it. The gleaming metal showed that a lot of care had been bestowed upon the object that lay before him. There was a saxophone inside it polished to perfection. He picked up the golden instrument and started playing a tune. There was a certain zeal with which he played it. It felt as if he wasn't playing the saxophone but was making love to a woman and had an undying ardour to please her. The ringing of his landline made him stop abruptly akin to what a doorbell does to lovemaking. His dismay was evident from his suspiration. He picked up the phone placed on the nightstand next to him.

'Hello?'

'Yo Rehan, it's Arif.'

'Oh!'

'It's time to collect the cash. Meet me at the Colonel's house.'

'Yep.'

'Nine forty five, be there,' Arif said.

'Okay.'

Arif hung up the phone but Rehan was slow reacting. After a few seconds of hearing the dial tone, he hung up too. He looked at his saxophone which he had placed on the couch and shook his head in dejection. This was his reality. He was a contract killer on hire to answer to the beck and call of every nincompoop out there and that was all life had to offer him. Any dreams of normalcy he had would always die with one phone call.

He wiped and packed the saxophone back in its case and slid it under his couch. He went back into his bedroom and opened his almost monochrome closet. His black suits and ties hung on hangers on top. White shirts folded and layered on a shelf. One drawer held his wallet, keys, and watch while the other held other items of regular use. Besides his 'work' clothes, Rehan had little in the way of casual wear but all classy in its own way. Rehan wore the suit on and opened the right wall of his wardrobe that had a concealed panel. There it was, all shiny, silver and attractive. Rehan knew that it was as lethal as it was beautiful, almost feminine in its attributes but definitely masculine in its approach. He picked out the AMT Harballer pistol with its silencer, shoved it into his coat pocket and made his way out of the apartment.

8th June 2013
Bandra, Mumbai

'The stock market crashed again. I had a fortune running on my HDFC stocks. My wife is going to be very disappointed that we won't be making the trip to Europe this year too.' Rehan overheard a man say to his colleague overemphasizing on the "too", as he went over the daily news on his cell phone.

He had boarded the local train at the Victoria Terminus and was on his way to Bandra to meet the Colonel. He savoured travelling in the Mumbai locals. The way in which he could blend in with the crowd and become invisible to the world while travelling in these trains fascinated him. People from all walks of life travelled in them every day making their way to different destinations. No one gave a crap about who else was on board except when the elbows poking into ones ribs from all directions became too much to bear. The tolerance of a regular Mumbaikar was pretty high, perhaps because of the rush that hardly left space to stand on one foot and the unavailability of another means of transport capable of reaching destinations in reasonable amounts of time. Buses would take hours for what took minutes here and every Mumbaikar knew how much every minute was worth.

Thankfully the rush hours were now over and the train was relatively uncrowded.

'I hope it doesn't rain today. I absolutely hate getting home all wet.' Rehan heard another man say who was standing in the aisle. Over the years, Rehan had become adept in overhearing other people's conversation since he rarely had a companion and introspection wasn't as pleasurable for him as much as it was for others. He knew from the loudness of their voice how far they were from him. Always aware for any danger or threat, his senses never betrayed him. It came with his job. After all, there weren't a lot of people who carried a lethal weapon with them while commuting in public. Even though he kept a low profile, there could have been n number of reasons for anyone to get suspicious of him.

Rehan heard some bibulous laughter from behind him as the train pulled inside the Kings Circle station. Two men had just gotten on board and by the sound of their voice Rehan knew that they were totally liquored up. He could feel them getting closer to him as they indulged themselves in some mindless banter, which he cared not to decipher. He looked up from his cell phone and noticed that the girl sitting across him was looking directly at them, getting uneasy as the men drew nearer. She looked like a girl in her late teens and the satchel that she clutched onto suggested that perhaps she was on her way back home from college or tuition. Rehan saw the reflection of the men fall on her glasses and he perceived them to be two averagely built fellows in their early thirties. Rehan didn't conceive them as too much of a threat and went back to reading the news.

The men walked up in the aisle and stood right next to where he was sitting, their body emitting a strong stench of alcohol. The train was now on the move again. Rehan could hear the men whispering to each other as they stared at the girl lasciviously. The girl's body grew stiff; her anxiety now at its peak. She looked away, avoiding eye contact with the men.

'Oh man! She's a bomb.' One of the men said; his speech slurred.

'I like young girls, so innocent... so uptight,' said the other nudging his companion with a lopsided grin.

He then took a few steps towards the girl and stood right in front of her.

'Hello madam. What is the scene for tonight?' he said lewdly.

The girl still looked away and did not acknowledge the comment.

'Oye! Look at me when I am talking to you,' he said as he grabbed her face between his fingers and forced her to look at him, his one had clutching the railing above to maintain balance in his already delirious state.

'Are you scared? Look bro, baby is scared.'

'Back off,' said Rehan.

The men turned around. They saw Rehan engrossed in his phone.

'Did you say back off?' one man asked him.

Nothing...Rehan said nothing as he continued to look at his phone.

'No, he doesn't have the balls to say anything.'

'How can he?' said the other man. 'Look at him. Looks like some corporate douche bag dressed in formals, always prepared to get fucked.'

The men shared another sottish laugh.

'Back off,' Rehan said, 'before you get hurt.' He was still looking at his phone.

'Oh! And who is going to hurt us? You? Come on, go ahead.'

'Why don't you mind your own business and bugger off,' the man told Rehan.

'Why don't you?' Rehan joshed.

Angered by the back talk, the man went for Rehan's collar. Rehan caught his hand mid-air, pulled him closer and head butted him right in the face. The man recoiled back holding his nose and wincing in pain. The other man charged at Rehan and threw a punch. Rehan sidestepped and dodged it; the man caught the metal of the bench. Three jabs in the face in quick succession and the man's nose was bloodied. The other man tried attacking but Rehan blocked his strike and elbowed him in the throat with his left hand. Then he grabbed his head and drove it into a holding bar in the aisle. The man fell to the ground unconscious, bleeding from his skull. The other man grabbed Rehan around his neck from the back, trying to choke him. Rehan stomped powerfully on his foot once, which made him loosen the hold. Rehan then drove his elbow into the man's abdomen. The man bent down holding his stomach, gasping for breath as his insides threatened to escape down the wrong lane. Rehan held his head and crashed it against his upcoming knee before delivering a violent chop to the back. The man dropped to the ground on his belly bleeding from his nose and mouth.

All this had barely lasted a couple of minutes and the train was pulling into Mahim station. Rehan looked down at the bodies of the men who lay unconscious on the floor in the narrow passageway. A pool of blood lay around them soaking into their clothes. He closed the palm of his right hand in a fist, making him wince. His knuckles had been bruised. It was only a few seconds later that he realised that all the eyes in the train were drawn on him as the train slowed to a halt. A ticket collector had boarded the compartment. He saw everyone looking at a bloodied man; shell shocked. What Rehan hadn't realised was that during the brawl, his pistol had slipped out of his coat pocket and was now resting on the floor near his legs. The train whistled and began chugging along. Rehan saw the ticket collector get off in a rush. He then slowly picked up the AMT Hardballer handgun and plunged it into his pocket before returning to his seat, his actions running more on reflex than on thought.

The bogie had gone all quiet. After all, people didn't witness a brawl on the train every day. Rehan looked up at the girl. She looked frightened but she also seemed a little grateful.

'Thank you,' she said softly.

Rehan gave her an acknowledging nod. But her gratitude wasn't something he was worried about. Nor did the people's fright bother him. He knew there would be repercussions for his actions and that he would have to be very careful. Within a few minutes the train would arrive at the Bandra station and there was a high possibility that the cops would come looking for him. He was sure that the ticket collector would have relayed the information to the next station and that only meant trouble for Rehan. Why did he have to pick up the gun? He could have as easily claimed that the thugs had it concealed and he was sure the girl would have corroborated. But it was already done; he couldn't waste another moment on what could have been.

Rehan sent a quick text message from his phone, got up and stood at the exit of the compartment. He could see the next station approaching in the distance. He gathered his composure and wiped the blood off his hands on the lining of his trouser pockets. The train had pulled into platform number five of the Bandra Terminus. Rehan got down from the train as it slowed and started walking quickly towards the opposite platform, searching for some place to change his garb. He wanted to buy as much time as possible to make an escape quietly. He swept the platform for signs of cops, none yet. He made his way into the washroom and entered the cubicle. Rehan got out of his coat and shoved it into the cistern of the toilet. He tucked his shirt out, folded his sleeves halfway and sheathed his pistol under his belt. He then threw away the tie and opened his collar button.

Knowing how the cops in India were highly incompetent and challenged in the weapons department, he knew that there wouldn't be a whole task force out there to get him. Four or perhaps five cops must be on the lookout for him; that is what he predicted. He knew that getting past them would not really require any grandiose plans. The more low-key his escape, the better it would be. He washed his hands in the sink and tried to get rid of whatever blood was left on them. The bruises were now beginning to hurt him. After splashing some water on his face, Rehan got back on the platform and started walking towards the overheard bridge as casually as possible.

There were four policemen standing on platform number five as Rehan had expected. Three of them were lower ranking officials and carried nothing but bamboo sticks as weapons. The fourth one was an inspector. Rehan saw him talking on his walkie-talkie as he continued to move along platform number four. There was a pistol hanging on his belt. Rehan quickened his pace. If he could make his way out of the station without being noticed, he would be safe. He heard footsteps behind him.

'Hey you! You in the white shirt,' he heard someone behind him. 'Stop right there.'

Rehan stopped, his eyes scanning the surrounding through the sunglasses.

'Good. Now put your hands where I can see them.'

Rehan raised his hands and placed them behind his head. His heart was now beating faster, his thoughts running helter-skelter, searching for a feasible get away. He heard the footsteps approaching him.

'Now turn around nice and easy.'

Rehan turned around as a train pulled into the station on the platform next to him. He saw the inspector standing some twenty metres away with his pistol pointed straight at him.

'Search him up,' the inspector told the other cops.

'What have I done?' Rehan said in protest feigning ignorance.

The cops walked right towards him without answer. More solicitous than he had ever been, Rehan knew he had to make a run for it. If they got to him, he was going down. But where could he run to avoid getting shot. Running along the platform was no good. Other people had drifted away from him so he couldn't take anyone as a human shield. He was definitely not going to open fire on the cops, for that would make him a marked man for life. Then he heard the words 'Blood… back' in a conversation a few paces behind him, which suddenly made the situation clear as to what had aroused suspicion. In his hurry, he had forgotten to check the back of his shirt, which apparently had bloodstains. He cursed under his breath.

The cops were merely ten metres away.

Rehan heard the horn of a train go off. The train next to him had started moving. Rehan moved his hands and raised them over his head taking a step to his left, the cops now standing right in front of him. One of them bent down and started running his had hands over Rehan's pants. The train had now gathered enough speed and getting on it was near impossible. As the cop's hands reached his belt, Rehan spread out his left hand towards the moving train. He caught the moving railing on the entrance of a bogie and flew off the platform in a jerk. He pulled himself into the train, ran towards the other exit and jumped off the moving train. Rehan took a few tumbles on the platform before getting back up on his feet. The train had blinded the cops on the other side of the platform. He made a sprint towards the exit of the station leaping over platforms and railway tracks. He turned around as he reached the outlet doors; the cops were running towards the overhead bridge. The next arriving trains were approaching fast, making jumping the tracks unsafe. About three minutes, that was the time the cops would take to reach him as they made their way through the crowd. Three minutes were more than enough for him to disappear.

Rehan got out on the street and walked hastily towards the market place. His plan was simple. He wanted to gel with the crowd so detecting him would pose a problem to the cops. In another minute he would reach the market and then just vanish out of thin air.

Rehan heard sirens and honking of horns. He turned around to see a police SUV heading towards him.

'Oh shit!' he said breaking into a dash again.

Rehan hadn't seen this coming. He could no longer stay on the road and he needed a change of clothes, fast. He moved on to the pavement and barged through the crowd. Seeing him running from the cops, a few people tried to block his way but Rehan tackled them and knocked them over in the process. The SUV was right on his tail and he knew that a detour was necessary, but first he had to change lanes. He saw a skywalk in front of him. It was always better to be chased by the cops on foot than by the cops on wheels but a skywalk was an enclosed area and he wasn't planning to get trapped in such a place.

Glancing behind to take a look at the traffic, he dashed across the road, jumped over the fence on the divider and crossed the road to temporary safety. He saw the SUV stop as two police constables got down from the vehicle and headed up the skywalk to cross the road as the SUV moved on looking for a U-turn.

Typical, worthless bums. He had a hundred metre head start over the constables who were chasing him and the SUV would take its time and he wasn't about to give up his leverage to another mistake.

To his right he saw a low house and with one foot on the window grill, grabbed the ledge on the building. He pulled himself up with all his strength and got himself on the roof. Seeing the physical condition and age of the constables chasing him, he knew they wouldn't be able to follow him up there when they couldn't even cross the road. He started running in the opposite direction pulling out the gun as it was biting into his back. The roof was narrow and curving; his foot slipped which almost made him fall off. He held on to the ledge with his hands and got back on his feet and climbed a few more ledges to maintain height as it always gave one the vantage point for a better view of the surroundings. Ahead, he could see a gap in the buildings as if a lane was cutting through. He increased his pace and just before the end of the roof, leaped off the house, over the lane and on to the terrace of another building, landing on his hands and knees. The trauma of the landing wounded his left knee and he cringed in pain. He got back to his feet and limped to the parapet of the terrace. Another rooftop was close by; he jumped onto it taking a few tumbles.

Rehan turned around and looked down at the road, crouching down behind the breastwork. The rozzers were making their way up the first building and he could see the silhouette of the first policeman helping the other alight against the streetlights of the main road. Rehan walked to the other side of the rooftop and saw a small dark alley running next to the building lit by a single naked bulb. There was a pipeline running straight down the two storied establishment he was on. Rehan wrapped his hands and legs around the pipe and slid down as the cops got up to the terrace. They didn't see him and to further ensure his escape, he pulled out his handkerchief and unscrewed the bulb instantly immersing the lane in complete darkness.

He followed the lane to circle back towards the railway station trying to get the policemen off his scent: the unexpected was a fugitive's best ally. Rehan shoved his AMT Hardballer handgun back into his trousers and moved back onto the road. He made his way to the rickshaw stand.

'Hill road,' he told the auto rickshaw driver.

The rickshaw had to pass along the main road, which made Rehan anxious. He leaned back into the vehicle and covered his face with his hand subtly as they drove past two police inspectors and the SUV.

❚ ❚ ❚

The rickshaw was now riding along Hill Road. Rehan breathed a sigh of relief realizing that his escape was complete. He had conceptualized the Mumbai Police very wrongly today, they had acted faster than he expected. They had really come at him hard and his injured knee was proof of that. But the heart of his prevision still remained standing; the police in India were incompetent and today was also a proof of that.

Rehan asked the rickshaw driver to pull over next to the Saint Andrews Church. He paid the fare, got down and started hobbling along towards Mehboob Studios. A nice breeze had started blowing and his soaked shirt made him shiver a bit as he walked down the road lit in yellow towards the back of the studio. The weather was taking a turn towards the good, and it felt like one of those nights on which you just want to sit in an open air restaurant and enjoy a nice drink with someone special. Thinking about such things took his mind off his job and it was good to function mechanically at times. As he approached the back gates of Mehboob Studios, he saw the black Chevrolet sedan parked right next to it. He walked to it, knocked on the passenger window and got inside.

'Why did you text me and ask to pick you up here?' Arif said. 'I was supposed to pick you up at the station twenty minutes ago.'

'I ran into some trouble,' said Rehan.

'What kind of trouble? And where is your coat?'

Rehan shrugged at the question 'Forget it man, nothing special.'

'I see the bruises on your hand, you stink like a pig and you aren't wearing your coat. Don't tell me you got caught up with the cops.'

Rehan looked out of the window coldly.

'Motherfucker, you did get involved with the cops,' Arif said. 'So what, you beat them up? Please don't tell me you shot them.'

'No goddammit, I did not shoot anyone. Now can you please shut the fuck up and drive.' For the first time in his life, Rehan had put himself and the company in jeopardy and he wasn't very happy about it. He opened the glove box of the car and picked out a packet of cigarettes. He lit one and took a long drag at it. This wasn't really helping him either.

'So are you going to tell me what happened?'

'No,'

'Then I wonder what the Colonel will have to say about this.' Arif said as he started the engine of the Chevy.

'Since when did you become so perfidious?' asked Rehan

'Perfi...what?'

'Never mind, some of us do have a vocabulary beyond just knowing all forms of fuck.'

'Dude what the fuck is wrong with you?' said Arif resting his hand on Rehan's shoulder.

'I don't know man. I think I seriously need a break.'

'Okay. Let's go and talk to Puri. Considering your encounter with the cops today, he might ask you to lie low for a while,' said Arif as they zoomed off in the black sedan.

8th June 2013
Bandra, Mumbai

Colonel Puri sat in his armchair looking at the portrait above the fireplace mantle as a blazing red fire roared in front of him.

'Are you sure you weren't followed here?' He asked after Arif broke the news of Rehan being pursued by the cops to him.

'Yep, we are pretty sure,' Arif said.

The Colonel took a sip of the scotch from the glass he held.

'Pretty sure isn't good enough. You need to be absolutely sure,' he said.

'I lost them around the station itself. There is no need to panic. The situation was contained,' Rehan chipped in. 'Also, isn't it hot enough already?'

'You say the situation was contained, huh?' the Colonel said choosing to ignore the quip as he looked at Rehan over his shoulder. 'What I want to know is how did this situation arise in the first place?'

Rehan walked over to the bookshelves and absently browsed through the books.

'Well...there was an incident on the train,' he said.

'An incident, ha! If you could elaborate on that incident, it would be great, Mister Irani.' The Colonel was evidently a little irked by Rehan beating around the bush.

'Let's put it this way…I beat the living shit out of two guys on board and dropped my weapon.'

'And why did we do that, may I ask?'

'That is irrelevant. What matters is that I got things under control.' Rehan said as he turned back and looked right back at the Colonel who was now standing by his study table.

'It matters to our company goddamit.' Colonel Puri thumped the table top with both his hands; his irritation totally visible. 'What part of keep a low profile don't you understand? You have worked for me for a while now. You know that if by any means the cops find out about us, we would be finished. And why the hell do you still travel by train? I pay you guys well enough. Why don't you buy a car?'

'Have I ever asked you why you sit in front of that stupid fireplace of yours and stare at that ridiculous picture every day?' Rehan blackguarded. 'So it would be better if you did your job and let me do mine the way I want. It's not that I did it on purpose. And I said the situation was contained, so will you just let it go?'

'Don't you dare talk to me like that.'

'Or else what? You will fire me? Go ahead and do that.'

'What the heck is wrong with this guy, Arif? How can he be so ungrateful after all that I have done for him?' the Colonel asked.

'What have you done for me?' Rehan retorted. 'Oh wait, I will tell you what you have done. You took my crappy life and turned it into a crappier one. Sure you took me off the streets and paid off my father's gambling debts after his death. But you have completely destroyed any chance of me leading a normal life. And if you think I should be grateful to you for that, then you can go screw yourself.'

The Colonel was fuming, staring Rehan down. The tension was almost palatable.

'Forgive him, sir,' Arif said trying to cool off the situation. 'He has had a rough couple of days.'

'No Arif, I want to know what his problem is,' said Puri. 'Ninety five lakhs; that is the amount of debt you were in when your father committed suicide. How were you planning to pay that off, Rehan? If it wasn't for me you would be sleeping in some gutter by now or worse come to worse…dead.'

'I'm not afraid of dying. We all have to die someday. What really bothers me is that I have to exist in a way that is as good as death,' Rehan said, his voice quivering. 'I can't have friends, I can't have love, and I don't have a family. What good is such a life? I am a college graduate. I am sure I could have found a decent job and worked my way out of that shit.'

'If you were so sure, then why did you accept my offer?' The Colonel said as he took his seat behind the desk. 'If you were so sure, then why did you let me help you?'

Rehan looked down at the floor blankly. He had no answer to that. No answers to justify his own actions.

'I will tell you why,' said the Colonel. 'Desperation! You were desperate, desperate to leave that life behind you and move on. You were desperate to finally get over an alcoholic gambling father who couldn't provide you with much of a childhood; desperate to quit grieving over your mother. You were desperate to get out of world where no one even knew you existed. Am I right?'

Rehan took a deep breath and tried hard to find something to say. He found nothing.

'I mean, look at Arif, he had a normal life, a normal job but yet, he could see his talents being used much more effectively here.' The Colonel paused briefly before continuing, 'But what really baffles me is why after so many days do you want to return to the life you so desperately wanted to give up on? Perhaps you have found something that reminds you of one of those rare happy days from your past? Or is it love? Please don't tell me its love.' Colonel Puri studied Rehan's face closely. He knew his question were making Rehan squirm, but one learns the most when the other is uncomfortable.

'Anyway, let's forget about this now. How did it go last night?' He said letting Rehan off the hook.

'It went very well,' Arif said. 'He was definitely ready to die. No regrets, I am positive of that.'

'What does that mean?' Rehan said as he looked at Arif coldly. Arif quickly wiped off the grin that had appeared on his face.

Colonel Puri briefly scanned both their faces and then picked up his glass of scotch. He made his way back to the fireplace and sat down in his armchair. Rehan picked out a cigarette and a lighter from his pocket.

'May I smoke in here?' he asked Puri.

'Don't you know smoking kills?'

'Apparently I kill too,' Rehan muttered and lit the cigarette taking a puff from it.

'Demimonde...do you guys know what that word means?' The Colonel said as he stared at the portrait in front of him. No one answered him. 'It is used to describe a group of people who are involved in activities that are ethically or legally questionable. It is mainly used for prostitutes. Now I know you think we fit that description well. But today I want to tell you the truth behind the Greener Pastures Company. Why don't you guys take a seat?'

Rehan and Arif looked at each other, shrugged and took their seats in front of the desk. Colonel Puri turned in his armchair to face them.

'What if I were to ask you what you did for a living?' He asked Rehan. 'What would your answer be?'

'Do you want me to tell the truth or are you asking me what I would say if someone asked me that?' Rehan said.

'I want to know what you think you do for a living.'

Rehan took one last puff from his cigarette and stubbed it in an ashtray placed on the desk. 'I kill for a living. I am a hitman.'

'See now that is where you are mistaken, my boy,' the Colonel said. 'Sure you kill for a living, but you are not a hitman.' He took a sip of his scotch and continued. 'Arif knows about this but I have never told you because firstly, you never asked me, and secondly, I didn't think it would make any difference to you. But today when I see you doubt your life, I think that maybe if I tell you about our Company, it might just make you feel a little better about your job. You see this picture that I keep staring at every day. This was my son Vikram. I was posted in Himachal and he was just fourteen. That was when he was diagnosed with leukaemia... blood cancer. Two whole years of chemotherapy and still he did not get any better. When the doctors finally weaned him off the chemo, he hardly had a few months left. The toxic drugs and the disease had taken a toll on him so badly that he couldn't move, couldn't talk, couldn't eat. All he did each day was stare outside into the woods from his window with those lifeless eyes on that pale face waiting for death to embrace him. But it did not. It was almost cruel and I could not take it anymore. On 15th December 2007 at twenty one hundred hours, I took him into those woods and... shot him in the head with my service revolver.'

The forest was back again, the fresh air, the cold metal turning hot in an instant as a tongue of fire turned everything to red and then nothing except his own howls. A teardrop rolled down Colonel Puri's moist eyes. 'I loved him, he knew that. I freed him from his misery, I am sure he knows that too. Those years changed me as a person. I could no longer live the life of an army officer; no longer live the life of a man. I couldn't stand to see the pain of people dying such useless deaths. So I quit the army and moved to Mumbai and decided to help anyone who couldn't wait for their own death. After my sister Priya married Arif, I told him about my vision and he joined me.'

The Colonel took a deep breath and steadied himself. 'Now comes the hard part. Arif had heard about you from a moneylender and knew about your debts. We wondered why you would like to stay alive after all that had gone wrong with you. So I approached you. If I would have failed to recruit you then...'

'Then you would have killed me,' Rehan filled in.

'That was a possibility.'

'That would have been nice,' Rehan said. A smirk crept up on his face

'So what I really want to tell you is that you don't kill people for me or anyone else. You kill them because they themselves want to die. Euthanasia...that's what they call it nowadays,' the Colonel said.

'They have been calling it that for a long time now,' Rehan said as he took out another cigarette from his pocket and lit it.

'That's not the point. The point is that whether after knowing this you feel better or not.'

'Colonel, I don't think there is a person in this world who would feel better after killing a man.' Rehan got up on his feet, 'But yeah, knowing that the money I make isn't stained with an innocent but a helpless man's blood is quite relieving. What I don't understand is why would anyone pay a fortune to get himself killed. It's almost stupid. Why not just jump off a building or slit your wrist or something.'

'Have you ever thought about killing yourself?' the Colonel asked. 'The whole idea is scary as fuck. You need a lot of courage to jump off a building Rehan, and that is something not everyone has.'

'Hmm…anyway, I think that we are done here then. Can we just please get our money and get out of here?' Rehan was truly disgusted about what he had just heard but still he was trying hard to make himself believe that he was doing his victims a whole lot of good.

'Your money is kept in that briefcase by the door,' the Colonel said. 'And there is an envelope on my desk, pick it up. Inside it you'll find the address of your next target. You are to enter at 2:16 a.m. day after tomorrow. The back door will be open. Be as humane and quick as possible.'

'Thank you, sir,' said Arif. 'We also have Mr. Fernandez's laptop. What should we do with it?'

'Break it and throw it in the ocean.'

'Sure sir.'

'Oh, and Arif, how many months are left for Priya's due date?' the Colonel asked.

'She is in her seventh month now. Two more to go.'

'You better be taking care of her.'

'Well, what can I say? When you're in love, you're in love,' Arif said.

Rehan laughed slightly after hearing this. Arif turned around and stared at him furiously. Rehan took a drag from his cigarette as he looked at Arif and Colonel Puri glaring at him. Both of them were waiting for an explanation.

Rehan's smile quickly faded, 'Sorry…thought of something else.'

Arif picked up the briefcase on their way out as both of them made their way out of the bungalow and headed towards Arif's Chevy parked in the driveway.

'That went well I think,' Arif said.

Rehan shrugged as he got into the car.

'Hey come on, at least we got to learn a new word. Now my vocab has something except just different forms of fuck.' Arif winked turning the ignition on. 'Demigrondy…We are both demigrondys brother.'

'It's Demimonde. And it is used for a group so it is a plural form in itself.'

'Who gives a flying fuck about that man? Let's go get ourselves a fucking drink,' Arif said as they vroomed off along Carter road.

Prostitutes… the Colonel is right about us, thought Rehan as lights zoomed by unfocused.

A group of well-dressed people were walking or rather swaying down the steps that led to a huge door topped by bright red neon saying "Red Light Club". They were laughing and obviously inebriated. A small line of people stood outside the door, to the side, waiting to be admitted.

Rehan and Arif sat at the bar counter on adjacent chairs as they looked out over the dance floor. Both of them held bottles of Corona.

'So, are you scouting the area?' Arif yelled through the near deafening house music playing in the club.

'Nope, I'm just enjoying my drink,' said Rehan.

'You can be honest. I won't judge you.'

Rehan ignored the comment and took a small sip of his beer. Arif's eyes widened and he nudged Rehan's shoulder.

'What?' asked Rehan.

Arif pointed through the crowded dance floor at the dimly lit silhouette of a woman standing against a wall in a beautiful green dress. She caught Rehan's eyes as he cowardly turned away, breaking the connection.

'Dude, you better go talk to her,' said Arif. 'I'm not fucking around. She is gorgeous. Hell, if you don't go, I might have to.'

'Aren't you married?' asked Rehan rhetorically.

'Okay, yeah I am married. But I can still feast my eyes. It's not like I masturbate to my seven month pregnant wife.'

'Oh, then who do you think of?'

'Robert Fucking Pattinson. Fuck you,' Arif said as he put his drink down and looked at Rehan in all seriousness. 'Don't you get bored man, lonely? I have to drag you out, you're not social. What in the fuck is it? Do you enjoy being alone?'

'Didn't you get anything out of my babbling today?' Rehan said. 'Of course I don't like being alone, but then such is our job. It's been making me crazy. I try hard to tell myself that I'm not lonely.'

'Well, tonight you sure as shit won't be lonely.'

Rehan looked at Arif all confused. Arif stood up and grabbed his drink. He walked through the dance floor towards the woman in the green dress. Rehan saw him talking animatedly with the girl. She looked over as he pointed at Rehan. *The bastard,* thought Rehan, *always making a mess* as he gave them a half assed wave. Within a few seconds, the two of them started walking over towards the bar. Rehan grabbed his beer and downed it. Arif and the girl arrived and took their seats on either side of him. The girl was looking right at him.

'Hey, I'm Aneesha,' she said

'Rehan,' he said shaking her hand.

'Well, I'm just going to head out and let you two talk,' said Arif. He got up, took his coat and silently whispered into Rehan's ears before walking out, 'Your mom just died.'

❚❚❚

Aneesha and Rehan shared a couple of drinks before taking a cab back to Rehan's apartment. She sat down on the couch and crossed her legs. Rehan turned on the lights, opened two bottles of beer from the fridge and walked over. He sat down opposite her.

'So, what exactly is it that you do?' she asked after taking a sip of her beer.

'I am a business analyst for a small firm but I don't really like talking about my job,'

'Why? Are you ashamed of it? Because it seems whatever you do, it pays,' she laughed and pointed around the bland apartment.

Rehan merely gave a pained smile and sipped his beer. 'You know how expensive it is to keep up this appearance?' he laughed.

Aneesha was one step ahead as she chugged her beer in seconds. 'So why don't you elaborate on that in your room?'

'I am sorry. But I don't feel up to it,' he said as he took out the crumpled picture from his pocket and stared at it.

Aneesha got up from her place and took a seat next to Rehan. 'Is she your girlfriend?' she asked after looking at the picture.

'No, she is just someone I used to know.'

'So what do you suggest we do?' She stirred and rested her hand on his back. He flinched slightly.

'You don't mind if I go out for a smoke, do you?' he said and walked out onto the balcony. Rehan sat on the chair in his balcony with a cigarette in his hand. He watched over the darkness trying to ignore the yellow snaking lights and was partly at ease. The other part was occupied thinking about the almost twenty minutes he had already spent here ignoring the girl. He took another long drag. The door slid open, Aneesha stood in the door frame. Her dress was now off. She had a blanket wrapped around her apparently naked body.

'Can I bring out a chair?' she asked.

Rehan merely shrugged. She smiled back and carried out a chair from the living room. She sat next to him and looked out at the cumulus of shining towers seen in the distance.

Aneesha took the cigarette from Rehan and puffed on it. 'You don't like company, huh?' she asked.

'What gave you that impression?'

'Well, apart from the obvious, you only got one seat on your balcony.'

He nodded and took a deep breath, then turned to her. 'I come out here a lot. To get away, you know. So an empty seat... it wouldn't feel right.'

She leaned back in her chair. 'You haven't dated in a while, have you?'

'You ask a lot of questions, don't you?'

'I always find that people, who don't talk much, need to talk the most.'

'How would you know, if they didn't talk much?' Rehan quipped.

She tried to stifle her laugh. 'Okay, last question, I promise. Have you ever been in love?'

Stupid question. Who among my age hasn't?

'I don't know,' he said. 'I never understood the definition of love. It's used too loosely.'

'Hmm,' she said and paused for a while before continuing. 'I think I should get going now. It's getting late. It was a pleasure meeting you. Also, my dress looked better on me than this blanket.'

Rehan looked into her eyes deeply. 'I'm sorry,' he said.

'For what?'

'For tonight,' he said pointing across her blanket covered body.

'Well, so am I,' she said and planted a kiss on his cheek. 'I will let myself out. Thanks for the drinks.'

Aneesha left the balcony and closed the door behind her. Rehan heard the front door being shut a couple of minutes later. He saw her exiting from the main gate of the building. She hired a cab and drove off. Rehan went back into the living room, turned the lights off and fell down on the couch. He took off his shoes and socks and slid them under the couch. He unzipped his pants and tossed them off. Now lying down on the couch in his dirty white shirt and boxers, he switched on the television and flipped through the channels. The picture of T.V Fernandez appeared on the screen.

'The death of Mister Tony Vivian Fernandez has now been ruled a burglary and homicide,' said the newscaster. 'Although there are no suspects as of now…'

Rehan remembered his mother, how she used to sing to him on such sleepless nights. It had been years since he had heard her voice. Cancer had taken her too early in Rehan's life to actually be able to feel the presence of a mother beyond what could be gained from the bedside. It was in his 8th grade that she had finally succumbed to the disease that had eaten away at her till whatever was left couldn't even speak his name. Its prolonged effect had left a lasting impression of the impermanence of everything in life which was refuted only later by the permanence of strife.

They were already in debt and then his Dad took the opportunity to drink more than ever, gamble away any chance of leading a normal life ever again until the weight of it all finally crushed him leaving his only son to carry forward his legacy of pain and debt on his young shoulders. He had the physical strength but not the psychological prowess to get away from the mess. That was till a helping hand pulled him out of the mire. But no, watching the blood on the rocking chair, he realized that he had made a pact with the devil instead of trying for a place in heaven.

Rehan flipped the channels and continued until he got to the Animal Planet. A soft music played in the background as a cheetah guardedly stalked his prey. Rehan lit another cigarette, leaned back and kept watching the show with a face devoid of emotions. Even the cheetah couldn't run for long…

10th June 2013
Airoli, New Bombay

The houses in this part of the city looked shadier than what Rehan was used to. Arif's sedan was parked outside a rundown housing complex. Graffiti littered the compound wall of the building, quoting slogans of a political party. It was almost time for the next hit.

Arif sat in the driver's seat and looked up at the building.

'I hate, fucking hate doing hits in society complexes. It's way too risky man,' he said.

'Yeah, I know,' said Rehan.

There was a moment of silence. Arif looked at his watch. It was 2.05 a.m.

'So you hit that shit?' he said changing the topic.

Rehan smirked. 'No, I didn't hit her.'

'Come on man, you know what I mean,' said Arif.

'Yeah, I know what you mean,' said Rehan. 'And no, I did not have sex with her.'

Arif flinched a little and then recovered. 'When you say it like that, it sounds so slimy.'

'Whatever.'

'But why didn't you do it?'

'It just didn't feel right,' said Rehan.

'Why? Was she hairy? Tits uneven?' asked Arif intriguingly.

'It might be the fact that you told her my mom died, you sick fuck,' said Rehan.

'You should have fucked her man.'

'And that doesn't sound slimy?' asked Rehan. 'Never mind, let's just get on with our damn job which, if not more, is as slimy.'

Arif nodded a few times and looked out of the window. He then checked the time again. It was 2.12 a.m.

'Should we go?' asked Rehan.

'Yeah.'

They exited the car, and walked nonchalantly to a break in the wall they had noticed while circling the compound.

Jumping over the wall of the complex, they crouched low in the shadow of the wall and looked for signs of movement. Smoothly then, they made their way towards Row House Number five. They took the small alley behind the row of identical houses and stopped at the fifth door. The door was slightly ajar but there were no telltale lights showing occupancy. They got inside and shut the door behind them. The room was small and cluttered, apparently by the dark shapes hugging each other. It was pitch black inside, except for a sliver of light coming from a room with the door closed. With muffled steps they moved towards the room. Rehan drew out his pistol and pushed the door open.

A girl was lying belly down on the floor next to the bathtub. She wore a black tank top and white shorts. Her curly hair were falling on her face covering it. She was clearly unconscious.

Arif stepped into the bathroom casually while Rehan stayed back along the wall. There was a tattoo of a butterfly on the girl's right calf, just above the ankle. Rehan spotted it. Confusion creased his face.

Arif checked the pulse: weak but steady. He then slowly pulled out his gun and cocked it. He pointed it at her head. His finger was ready to pull the trigger when…

'Stop!' Rehan interrupted.

Arif turned around; Rehan was rooted to the spot.

'What? She's clearly fucked. Let's get this shit over with man,' he said.

Rehan was breathing heavily. He scrambled backwards, slipping and adjusting himself on the sink ledge. He then kneeled in front of the unconscious girl, kept his gun down and took a closer look at her face.

'What the hell is going on?' Arif asked.

'It's her man, it's her.'

'Calm down man. You're fucking with my brain,' Arif said running his hand over his face.

'We can't kill her, we just can't,' said Rehan as he peered into Arif's eyes.

Arif was in shock, his mouth slightly askew. He stared at Rehan and Rehan watched the young woman lying on the floor.

'Have you gone out of your mind? This is our job!' He said.

'No, it's her, it's her,' said Rehan with his usual dexterity of words as he raised her head and brushed the hair aside. Her face could now be clearly seen. Through all the pain, she was beautiful.

Arif dropped his gun and knelt down next to Rehan. Together they picked her up and took her to the bed whose edge could be seen by the bathroom light escaping the open door. She was still unconscious, her head lolling from side to side. They laid her down on her side with arms and legs at right angles then Rehan sat next to her checking her breathing and pulse again, opening her mouth to search for blocks in the throat while Arif turned on the light. Rehan reached into his pocket and pulled out the crumpled picture. His hands shook as he un-crumpled it. It was obvious that the girl in the picture was a younger version of the girl who lay next to him. She still had those curly brown hair and that almost perfect nose which Rehan remembered so well. He could almost see her hazel eyes through the partly open eyelids, more green than hazel, he remembered.

'Sasha…Sasha,' he said as he ran his hand over her marmoreal skin and then covered her with a blanket that lay at the foot of the bed.

'I'll ah…wow…I'll go and tell the Colonel,' said Arif. He was still in complete disbelief. 'Wow, this is a fucked up situation.'

Arif walked out the door but not without a number of glances back at the still scene of Rehan sitting next to the unconscious Sasha.

Rehan caressed her head for a while as he studied the room which, besides a bed, and dressing table littered with cosmetics had a closet that was threadbare and a chair covered with a heap of clothes. After switching off the lights in the room he returned to the living room where a rather anxious Arif was pacing up and down, trying to make a phone call.

'The Colonel isn't picking up the phone man,' he said.

'I think we should leave,' said Rehan. 'We will go meet the Colonel first thing in the morning.'

'We can't just leave man… I mean what about this fucking job?'

'This job isn't happening tonight.'

'Dude…this girl wants to die. She has paid a fortune for that. Who are we to change that?' said Arif.

'Well she isn't dying today. And there isn't a goddamn person who can change that. Is that understood?' Rehan frowned.

'Yeah…okay.'

'So let's get out of here,' said Rehan.

They made their way out of row house number five via the back door in the kitchen, jumped the compound wall right opposite the house, never going back the way they came in, and got back into the car. Rehan looked back at Sasha's house as Arif started the vehicle. He just couldn't wrap his head around the fact that she wanted to kill herself. After all this wasn't anything like the Sasha he knew some seven years ago. But then the Sasha seven years ago didn't have her father's head blown off a day before. A lot of thoughts were racing through Rehan's head. Emotions from both extremes were wrestling each other. The past had begun reeling in front of his eyes and with every passing second, he found himself sinking into it.

'Some are born to sweet delight… Some are born to endless night.'

March 2003
Matunga, Mumbai

The farewell function of Ruia Junior College turned out to be quite a hit. This was the exact opportunity these oppressed depressed minds were looking for to vent their pent up steam. The graduating batch had had a gala time, probably for the last time before the exam schedule set in. Rehan made his way out of the main college entrance, his leather shoes crunching in the dirt, wearing his black tuxedo and bow tie. He chatted animatedly with the girl next to him who walked with one hand on his shoulder, walking precariously on high heels.

Women! he thought, but enjoyed the weight of her hand on him while he reflected how absolutely breathtaking she looked in the blue sari that she wore.

Rehan and Sasha had known each other for a long time now. They had first met in 6th grade and had remained good friends throughout school and junior college, which was evident by their level of comfort around each other. As she put her arm around his elbow, Rehan got goose bumps all over his arm. Over the years, he had developed strong feelings for Sasha. He had no idea when that had happened and no idea what he was going to do about it. But seeing her every day, talking to her and hanging out with her made him happy; he was content with that, for now. He, who had a highly fluctuating economic status with an unbalanced family setup already lopsided after the death of his mother had always been a kind of joke in school. And a girl as beautiful and popular as Sasha considered him to be her close friend was enough for him for the time being.

Rehan had always believed that Sasha was the prettiest girl alive and tonight after seeing her in a sari his belief had been reinstated irreversibly. He was completely mesmerized by her soigné appearance. She saw him looking at her.

'What?' she asked.

'You look wonderful tonight,' he said bringing Eric Clapton to aid his addled brain.

Her cheeks turned pink. 'Aww…Thank you. You are very sweet,' she said.

They made their way towards the Matunga Gymkhana. An after party had been arranged for their entire batch at the gymkhana by some juniors. Rehan had never been much of a party person. Walking on the pavements lit up by street lights with the girl of his dreams; this was where he wanted to be, talking where one could be heard, isolated from the senseless banter and inebriated gyrations that made the party scene of today. But he wasn't craw fishing out of it just because it meant spending more time with Sasha.

They entered a dimly lit party hall with shining disco balls and flashing strobe lights. The atmosphere in the room was electric and the music deafening; the exact reason why Rehan hated these flashy parties. One couldn't even see or listen to the other person clearly. Three girls rushed towards them from the dance floor. Rehan had no clue as to who they were but they seemed familiar. Everybody did in the dim light.

'Hey Sash…you are late,' yelled one of them.

'I am sorry babes. By the way, meet my friend Rehan,' Sasha said.

Rehan shook hands with the girls.

'Come on, let's hit the dance floor,' said the girl wearing a red top and a denim miniskirt.

'Sure, but I need to go change first. I can't possibly dance in this sari,' said Sasha. She then turned to Rehan. 'I'll be right back.'

Rehan saw Sasha go into the ladies room puzzled as she wasn't even carrying a change of clothes.

'You want to join us?' the girl asked him.

'No, I am going to wait here till she gets back,' he said.

The girls went back onto the crowded dance floor. Rehan went and occupied an empty table a couple of feet away from the DJ station who intermittently kept fisting the air as people in the club vied to copy his motions.

It had already been twenty minutes of waiting when he impatiently glanced towards the restroom only to see Sasha come out wearing a backless black dress which ended just above her knees and black stilettos which left his mouth hanging open for a second. He took a moment to gander at her as she walked towards him with measured steps.

'So, how do I look now?' she asked him.

'You look…nice,' Rehan said looking at her eyes. There was something different about her.

'Nice…Just nice? I thought you would come up with something more on the lines of hot and sexy.'

She stood just inches away from him and only a person with chronic respiratory tract infection could miss the strong smell of smoke her body and clothes emitted. But it did not smell like cigarette smoke. Rehan knew all about that. After all, his entire house was one big chimney, thanks to his father. Rehan peered into her eyes. Even through the dim lights he could see that they were bloodshot.

'Are you okay?' he asked her. 'Your eyes are red.'

'Don't be a bore Rehan. Tell me am I looking hot or not.'

'Very, but are you high? God, you smell awful,' he said.

'Well, that isn't very kind of you,' she said and walked two steps closer to him. 'But I forgive you,' she said running her hand through his hair. 'Now are you going to come and dance with me or what?'

'You know I can't dance. And looking at you, I think you shouldn't either,' he gently brushed her hand off of his head and moved back a little.

'I am perfectly fine,' she said and dug into her purse. She pulled out a joint from it. 'This is what I had and it isn't that bad. Haha... that rhymed,' Rehan stared at the long thin roll of translucent paper. 'I am feeling pretty good actually. Everything seems unusually slow and fun.'

'I will take that,' Rehan reached to take the joint from her hand

'No you won't,' she said pulling her hand away. 'What is your problem? Here I am, having a good time and you are trying to behave like my parent. What is with all this taking care of me business anyway? Firstly, you don't even have the balls to admit that you like me. And secondly, you are just too stupid to realize that I was trying to give you a shot to have me. But you know what...not anymore. It's done. I'm done with you.'

Sasha was fuming. Rehan was shell shocked. He had nothing to say to her. She was right, right about everything. He was a coward, a coward who could not fess up about his feelings for her. She turned away from him and started walking towards her friends on the dance floor. A feeling of self-loathing overtook Rehan as he saw her disappearing figure. At that moment he knew he had lost the girl of his dreams forever.

10th June 2013
Lower Parel, Mumbai

The Pegasus Estate was a forty-five storied commercial skyscraper and an odd phallic sight right in the heart of the city; it was one of the tallest buildings in Mumbai. Rehan and Arif sat on a couch in its lobby. A huge analogue clock hung on the wall right opposite them which showed the time as 10:10 a.m. like every watch in a store window does. This time always made Rehan feel static like those watches on display, and well it had been static for about two hours as they waited for the Colonel. Neither of them had managed to get any sleep following the events of last night.

Arif's anxiety levels were shooting through the roof. Never before in his life had he failed to complete an assignment. The Colonel was going to be very disappointed, perhaps furious too. He knew that.

Rehan on the other hand was least bothered about the wrath of the Colonel. He had other things perplexing him. All night long he had been trying hard to figure out why Sasha wanted to die. He was digging up the past, searching in the deepest recesses of his memories so that he could stumble upon a possible reason. He could think of none. He tried thinking about all sorts of permutations and combinations that could lead to a person making such a decision. After failing a couple of times, all he could come up with was the death of her father. It had to be that and he was responsible for it. All that guilt had started returning to him as he stared at the hands that had taken numerous lives almost glistening with red guilt

Arif made his way to the coffee machine placed on a table nearby. This was his sixth cup.

'We are fucked man, fucked I tell you,' he said.

Rehan saw no point in acknowledging Arif's obvious statement. He knew they were in a soup and the entire fault was his.

Colonel Puri walked into the building at half past ten, a folded newspaper in his hand. From the corner of his eyes he saw Rehan and Arif sitting on the couch. With a slight nod of his head he gestured them to follow him. They complied.

'Good Morning sir,' greeted the liftman as they entered the polished chrome elevator.

'Good Morning,' said the Colonel. 'Floor number forty-one please.'

'Certainly sir,' the liftman pressed the button numbered forty-one and they began ascending.

They walked along a long corridor on the forty-first floor crossing many corporate offices on the way. A wooden door at the end of the corridor had the words 'Greener Pastures Consultancy & Realtors' engraved on it in silver Monotype Cursive. Who could ever tell what really conspired inside? The Colonel had definitely left no stones unturned in the attempt of keeping the company's existence secret. They entered through the door into the waiting area of the Colonel's office. A female receptionist sat behind her desk playing minesweeper on her computer. She got up in a hurry on seeing the Colonel and the guys.

'Good morning sir,' she said.

'Any calls for me Aarti?' Colonel Puri asked.

'No sir.'

'Okay, carry on. And also, shift my other appointments by half an hour,' he said, gesturing at the two.

Colonel Puri walked past her into his cabin. Rehan and Arif followed him. The Colonel's cabin was almost an exact replica of his study except for the fireplace and the million books. Wooden interiors, a 1400's cartographic attempt at drawing the world hung on a wall while the completely explored version on a globe rested in a corner. An LCD screen on one side showed the feed from a CCTV camera placed in the reception and the corridor beyond. Rehan kicked himself for not noticing the cameras. A door led to what they presumed to be a bathroom.

'Please have a seat,' the Colonel said as he went over to the window to open the blinds.

The view of Mumbai's skyline from the window was splendid.

'Wow! The new office is amazing boss,' said Arif.

'Well thank you,' said Puri. After admiring the view from his window for a while, he turned around and saw Rehan sitting on a chair with a blank expression on his face, sunglasses on and a cigarette dangling from his mouth. 'Rehan, this is one place I don't really like people smoking in.'

Rehan walked over to the Colonel, opened the window and tossed his cigarette out. 'Sorry about that,' he said.

'So how did it go?' The Colonel asked.

'A minor problem occurred,' said Arif.

'What problem is that? Anything serious?' The Colonel took his seat.

'It... well, we didn't kill the target per se,' Arif said scratching the back of his ear.

'Didn't kill the target per se? What the hell does that per se mean? You paralyze her or something?'

'Umm...no, we...well Rehan more precisely didn't want to kill her,' said Arif nervously.

'What?' The Colonel exploded. 'I give you one goddamn job, carry it out and you get money, simple. Why the hell didn't you eliminate her?'

'Well we felt, or Rehan felt, per se, an attachment to the victim...sir,'

'What? Rehan you fell in love with someone who was about to kill herself,' said the Colonel. 'She is on the brink of death and you decide you're in fucking love?'

'It's not like that. I knew her from high school. I'm not in love,' said Rehan.

'So you two were a couple in high school? So what? You fooled around then, so you are fooling around now?' Colonel Puri asked angrily.

'No, we were good friends. That's it.'

'So you don't love her?'

Rehan shook his head in denial.

Colonel Puri sat in silence, pondering until finally he broke the silence and stared at Rehan intensely. 'So, you are actually serious about this? You don't want to kill her?'

'I can't kill her,' said Rehan.

'But she wants to die.'

'She thinks she wants to die.'

The Colonel nodded silently taking it in.

'Well, you have seven days to change her mind. Exactly one week from today I am going to ask her and if she still wants to die, I'll do it myself,' said the Colonel. 'Remember, don't let this love or whatever the fuck it is, mess everything up.'

'Thank you Colonel,' said Rehan as he shook Puri's hand.

'You can leave now.'

Arif and Rehan made their way out of the Colonel's office and made their way towards the elevator.

'So what are you going to do now?' Arif asked Rehan.

'I am going to go visit Sasha at her house today evening,' Rehan said.

'I don't think that's a very good idea. She hasn't seen you in seven years man. What will you say to her?'

'I don't know,' said Rehan. 'All I know is I have one week to change her mind and for that I have to meet her.'

'You want me to come with you?'

Rehan took out another cigarette as he leaned against the brick wall next to the elevator and lit it. 'No,' he said.

PART

II

THOSE SEVEN DAYS

10th June 2013

The evening sky was tinged in a shade of grey. The dense cloud cover prevented the setting sun from being seen, signs of a shower unmistakable. Rehan stood frozen in front of Sasha's house. Row House 5 – a plate on the door said, teasing him with the memories of last night as he crept in for the kill. The peeling white paint unnoticeable in the dark gave it a sad, almost destitute appearance. He didn't want to be here, of all the places. Why? Why was she living here?

All day long Rehan had thought of ways to present himself in front of Sasha, floundering as he tried to keep sleep at bay. If only he could in some way pass their meeting off as aleatory, that would have been great but sadly, this couldn't be passed off as a coincidence, he knew that. Rehan found no alternative but to come up front with all he had and hope for the best.

Rehan placed his sunglasses on his head, then decided to put them in his shirt pocket and faced the door impassively. His hand lingered on the door for a few seconds before he knocked it. His usually calm demeanour, even in the worst of situations was crumbling in the face of this ordeal. The door slowly creaked open. On the other side a small sallow face appeared as if disturbed from the recuperating sleep that would have brightened it up if not for him. It was messy and pained, yet beautiful. She blinked a couple of times at Rehan, who stood motionless.

'Rehan…is that you?' she said as if time had erased his being.

A smile crept up on Rehan's face. She remembered him, even if vaguely. 'Hi,' he said and waved back.

'Oh my god, what are you doing here?' she was definitely surprised evident by her wide eyed slack jawed expression.

'Nothing, I was just in the neighbourhood and thought I would drop by and see you,' he said, thinking *'Stupid! That didn't sound credible even to me.'*

'How did you know I stayed here?'

Valid point, he should have thought this through.

'Well, let's just say I like keeping track of my friends,' he said, trying to shrug it off coolly.

'Oh, do you now?' she asked rhetorically, teasing him.

Rehan nodded his head with a smirk on his face.

'Wow, it's been so long,' she said. 'I haven't seen you for like, what, eight years?'

'Seven.'

There was a moment of silence as they merely stared at each other, the rush of memories almost overwhelming.

'May I come in?' Rehan asked as he felt a raindrop fall on his head.

'Sure, I'll just change and be with you in five minutes,' she indicated by holding up five fingers as she let him into what could be called a living room but showed no signs of anybody living.

Rehan leaned on a wall across from the room Sasha had just entered. He analyzed the living room once again, its emptiness and homogeneity was evident. It did not look like a place where Sasha would stay. What had happened to her?

The door of Sasha's bedroom opened and she stood there with a hoodie and a tint of makeup on.

'You look swell,' he said.

She smiled back at him. 'I was wondering if we could go out somewhere, maybe for a walk.'

'I don't mind,' he said. 'But it is raining outside.'

'Oh it's just a little drizzle. There is a nice park close by. Let's go and sit there. The house is a mess anyway,' she said waving at what clearly was not how stereotypical women lived.

'Okay, sure.'

Sasha grabbed her house keys from the dinner table and put on her floaters. 'After all we have a lot of catching up to do,' she said.

'We sure do.'

❚ ❚ ❚

The breeze whipped her hair as she embarrassedly tried to keep them in check. Along with a slight drizzle, it was creating an atmosphere of utmost romanticism but sadly, Rehan had never been able to capitalize on such situations. The raindrops created ripples in the water of the pond in which many polliwogs swam freely. Rehan and Sasha sat on a bench in the park staring out over the pond. A few people were walking their dogs and the others were just strolling, but apart from that, the park was relatively empty.

Sasha spoke quietly, not taking her gaze away from the pond.

'Many a times I forget this park is even here.'

'Yeah, it's a nice place,' Rehan said.

He looked at her but her concentration was on the glassy

appearance of the water as it tried to reflect its surroundings but the drizzle always thwarted its attempts at clarity. She was obviously lost in thought, her expression troubled. A few seconds later she looked up at Rehan and let out a long sigh.

'You want to know something weird?' she said. 'I can't remember being young. It seems so long ago that I was a child, freewheeling. Life hadn't taken its toll yet, you know.'

Rehan didn't like where this conversation was going. It made him uncomfortable. 'Yeah, life...it gets tough, I guess,' he said talking from experience.

'So anyway, tell me what have you been up to lately?'

Rehan did not see any point in beating around the bush anymore. He was here to accomplish something and did not have a lot of time on his hands, also, any lies would be seen through immediately. She had known him long enough to decipher even the most cryptic messages he tried to throw at her.

'The Greener Pastures Company, have you heard of it?' he asked her.

He saw the expressions on her face change like the surface of the pond in front of him. She was completely blown out of the water, so to speak.

'I am sure you have,' he said. 'I am the guy who has been given the task to...eliminate you.' Those last words had been hard.

Sasha was patently scandalized. This wasn't something that she was expecting. How could she? A man she hadn't seen in seven years, a man whom she knew so well, had come up to her to tell her that he had been assigned to kill her. It took her half a minute to regroup. Finally she spoke.

'So, I bet you want to know why I want to die.'

'Not really.' Rehan said and took a brief pause. 'What I want to know is if you want to live.'

Sasha was surprised by his response. Rehan stared at her intently. She shuffled in her seat nervously and looked out across the water again.

'Sometimes, like right now, when my demons aren't chasing me into hiding,' she said.

Rehan pulled out a cigarette and lit it. He looked back at her and smiled slightly.

'And if these times were to extend, how about sometime in the future?'

❚ ❚ ❚

The stars looked like a collection of small LED lights in the sky. It was one of those rare monsoon evenings where the moisture and dirt did not coalesce to form dark clouds. Rehan and Sasha sat on the patio of Café Mocha in Juhu having their own pleasant rendezvous.

Rehan just couldn't take his eyes off her. He sat there simply captivated by her. Her serene beauty, her infectious laughter, the way she twirled the curls of hair with her fingers and the way she bit her lip gently when she got a little nervous; Rehan loved every bit of it. He loved every movement of hers, every sign of life. He did not want to live his life as an isolato anymore. He had blown his chance with her all those years ago; he was not going to blow it now. He would protect her; take care of everything that was bothering her; be the shield and the sword. They would start a new life together and he would make it happen.

He glanced across the terrace to see the road next to the café. Vehicles zoomed past his vision. In between that curtain of passing vehicles, he saw a figure of man standing on the opposite footpath. The man appeared familiar. He tried hard to get a good look at him but he was too far away. A couple of seconds later the rocketing stopped and he suddenly appeared on the sidewalk on his side. It was Colonel Puri. He stood there with his hands buried inside the pockets of his overcoat; his wrinkled face devoid of expressions, scrutinizing him with his bead eyes almost glowing in the dark. He slowly pulled his right hand from his pocket. Rehan saw him clasping onto a pistol which he slowly raised up, pointed it right at them; ready to pull the trigger.

'NO!' Rehan yelled and jumped out of his chair.

Rehan got up in a cold sweat and found himself sitting on his couch, panting and sweating profusely. Animal Planet was playing on his television as usual. He always watched the channel, maybe because their lives were led by simpler rules. Rules he wanted to live by, without thought, without regrets. As he moved, the gleam off his AMT Hardballer caught his eye as it lay on the coffee table. He was still in his trousers and shirt; his tie hanging loosely around his neck. It had been a dream; a rather bad one. Sasha was safe, or so he thought. His landline suddenly jumped to life, startling him. Rehan took a few deep breaths before answering it.

'Dude, what took you so long to answer the phone?' It was Arif.

'Ah, sorry I dozed off,' Rehan said.

'So are you ready or what?'

Rehan rubbed his eyes and yawned.

'Ready for what?' he asked.

'We have a job man. Didn't you get my text?'

'No, I didn't check. I was sleeping man.'

'So how long will you take?' Arif asked.

'Five minutes.'

'Okay, I am waiting for you downstairs.'

'Yep, I'm on my way,' Rehan said and hung up.

He went to the washroom and splashed some water on his face.

A stinging feeling overtook him as that cold water made contact with his sleep deprived eyes. After gargling with his mouth wash and brushing his hair he went back to the living room. He picked up his pistol and grasped it tightly. He removed the cartridge and examined it briefly before locking it back. Picking up his coat and sunglasses he made his way out of the apartment.

As opposed to his dream, it had been raining all evening. Arif's car was parked inconspicuously in the dead of night under a blown out street light. Rehan got inside and they started moving. He sat with his head leaning back against the car seat as soft music played from the car stereo, Coltrane with his sweet-sweet tunes. Arif knew how to please people at least.

'So, what's the news? Give me the lowdown man. You guys finally in love?' Arif asked.

'Huh?'

'Did you show her a good time?' Arif rephrased.

'It's not like that man. This isn't some lust thing.' Rehan said, 'I don't think I love her; I just want to save her.'

Rehan wasn't ready to admit his love for Sasha just yet. It seemed to him like a weakness; a weakness he had had all his life.

'Well. You got to at least love her a little if you want to save her.'

'Forget about it man. Tell me about the job. Where are heading?' Rehan asked.

'Well it is not far from here. Navy Nagar, some old dude with cancer,' Arif said. 'We will be there soon.'

🔫🔫🔫

Rehan and Arif walked out of the car and stood outside a small house lower than the surrounding multi–storey buildings.

From across the street, a light flickered on like a beacon in the dark. Arif took a look and turned around from the light abruptly, the silhouette of a woman clearly visible. His face had an evident look of panic. He knew it was a snafu but was by no means the first one they had encountered.

'Fuck!' Arif whispered.

'What?' Rehan asked.

'Little old neighbourhood aunty is staring right at us man.'

Rehan subtly tilted his head to have a look. An old lady stood at her window, in a sari even at this time of the night and stared intensely, squinting in the darkness at the dark shapes that was them.

'She can only see our back,' he said.

'She'll call the fucking cops man,' Arif was totally flipping out.

They looked at each other, obviously flustered by the current situation.

'Follow my lead,' Rehan said, knowing it was time for him to take the lead.

He walked casually to the door and opened it. Arif rushed in after him as the lady continued staring out of the window. Rehan immediately shut the door. Arif looked at him and nodded. He merely stared back at him.

'We have to make this quick man,' he said, then added, 'Don't worry, we could be visitors and the report of the gun wouldn't carry that far with these silencers.'

They saw the light at the end of a dark hallway and sneaked towards it. Arif had his gun cocked and pointed out in front of him. Rehan followed him closely. Arif kicked the door open and walked in to see a man staring at his TV. Rehan walked in, picked up the remote as the man quizzically looked at him and turned up the volume of the TV. The man turned briefly to look at Arif when without any warning he shot the man straight in the forehead with one bullet.

The background score of Top Gun and the battering noise of the rain soon engulfed the room as the men hurried out of the house. Sure that the report hadn't escaped the premises, they got out of the back door into a small kitchen garden, circled the compound and casually walked back to the car, small red lights illuminating two sets of fingers swinging nonchalantly.

11th June 2013

The midday sun wasn't the brightest and the grey cloud cover made the day rather gloomy; but thanks to the wind, the humidity wasn't that much of a trouble. Rehan and Arif sat in the waiting area of Colonel Puri's office. His receptionist Aarti sat behind her desk reading *Filmfare*. Reading about her favourite actors and actresses made her eyes glimmer hopefully. Perhaps she wanted to be like them and live their lives in the limelight rather than being stuck in a five by ten room with a desk job with these two buffoons as the only regular visitors to notice her. Rehan shuffled around on his seat. The chair wasn't really comfortable. The backrest and the cushion were inclined at a very atypical angle to his liking. Whatever happened to ergonomic design? Probably Mr. Puri wanted his visitors to squirm. An uncomfortable individual lets on more than he plans to.

'Would you stop that?' Arif objurgated getting irked by his constant movements.

'Sorry, is this bothering you?' Rehan asked.

'Yes it is. It looks as if your ass is on fire. Can't you just sit steady?'

'Wow, someone is in a mood today,' Rehan said. 'Why are you PMS-ing? Troubles on the home front?'

'What do you care fucker?' Arif retorted.

'Come on, you can tell me. It can't be that bad.'

'Man you have no idea what it is to deal with a pregnant female. They are so fucking moody. And those hormones, man those hormones make me feel like why the fuck did I get married in the first place?' Arif let out a long sigh. 'And this fucker,' he said pointing at the Colonel's cabin. 'Is he wanking inside or what? Been waiting here for twenty minutes man, twenty fucking minutes. And after all that, he wants me to spend more time with her. How man, how?'

Aarti looked up from her magazine and gave him a look of menace. Arif saw that and got a little embarrassed. 'Sorry,' he lip-synced.

A few minutes later a man in a neat navy blue suit walked out from the cabin. He hurried past them avoiding any eye contact with a briefcase in his hand.

He certainly doesn't look like he is dying. But then wanting to die had seldom had a relation with health, Rehan thought.

The intercom buzzed and Aarti dropped the magazine to pick it up in a hurry. A curt voice could be heard faintly from the other end as she kept the receiver down with a small 'Yes, Sir.'

'The boss will see you now,' she told them.

The men got up from their seats and headed inside. Colonel Puri sat behind his desk in a chair staring out over the city from the huge window.

'Hey guys please sit down,' he said not looking at them.

Rehan and Arif took their chairs and sat in front of him. Rehan pulled out a cigarette and put it in his mouth. He didn't light it but sat there silently looking at the Colonel. Colonel Puri finally turned around to face them.

'Do you mind?' Rehan said pointing at the cigarette, not taking his gaze off of the Colonel.

'No, I guess not,' he said.

Rehan lit the cigarette and sat there, drifting off into space. He let out a sigh of smoke, and leaned back against his chair.

'So, how's the love interest coming?' the Colonel asked. 'You saw her yesterday?'

'Yeah.'

'How did it go? What did you do on the first date?' he asked in an antagonizing manner.

'I took her to the park.'

The Colonel looked Rehan up and down, solemnly. He nodded and leaned in closer to the two of them.

'Did the kill go okay last night?'

'Yeah, I'll say. He was ready to go,' Arif said.

Rehan was zoning out.

'I'm taking her out again today.' He sighed absently. 'I just don't know where to go.' Immediately regretting what should have been an internal monologue.

'Nightclubs...Nightclubs always make me enjoy life,' Arif chipped in.

'What about being in my sister's presence?' The Colonel glared at him.

'Yeah that's number one...of course,' Arif said nervously.

'Of course,' said the Colonel.

'But, I couldn't give that advice to Rehan...could I?' said Arif with a smirk.

There was an awkward moment of silence. Arif suddenly wanted to bury himself in a hole as he felt those glaring eyes of the Colonel on him, his smirk fading in a jiffy.

'Well, you two make sure to stay low key for a while,' Colonel Puri broke the silence. 'Enjoy this week off. I have a couple of assignments but now isn't the right time. Now, if there is nothing else then you can show yourselves out. Your money is in the briefcase by the door.'

The Colonel turned his chair around and got back to looking out from his window. The two men got up and made their way towards the exit. Arif had picked up the briefcase and was already at the door, opening it with Rehan a few steps behind when the Colonel spoke again.

'Oh, and Rehan; it's day two.'

🔫🔫🔫

Rehan waited outside Sasha's room uncomfortably. His inner shirt was drenched with his own sweat. Taking the evening train from Victoria Terminal had been a rather bad idea considering the seventy-five per cent humidity. For forty-five minutes, he had just hung around the jam packed compartment, standing on one leg, dripping and now all of a sudden he wanted to cancel all programs for the evening. Going out on a fancy date with the girl of his dreams when he was perspiring like a pig didn't seem like a very good idea. During this whole phase of cerebration, he thought that maybe going to the park instead was a better option.

The door opened and Sasha stood there with a smile just at the edges of her lips. Such mischief dripped from them in accordance with the weather. They walked down the corridor towards the gleaming exit sign at the end of the hallway. Nothing but the faint echo of their footsteps could be heard before Sasha slammed the door shut.

'So where are we going?' she asked as they stood in her porch.

Rehan smirked back at her.

'Do you mind getting drenched?' He asked.

'Nope, I guess not.'

'So let's just go to the park if that's alright with you.' he said.

'Sounds good.'

▌ ▌ ▌

The park had been shut down as it was a good hour or two past its closing time but they had jumped the fence and entered nonetheless. All the lights had been switched off and the rain had become even more persistent. Neither Rehan nor Sasha had expected this. They rushed and took cover under a huge Pink Cassia tree planted at a corner. It provided a considerable shelter from the downpour. Rehan sat with his back against the trunk of the tree and Sasha lay down with her head in his lap, he could have lived a lifetime without thinking of moving an inch.

He took out a cigarette from his pocket and lit it as some rain drops tricked down the leaves of the tree and fell on them. Rehan took a puff and exhaled slowly, letting it fade into the night. Sasha held out her hand and took the cigarette from Rehan.

'You should see this tree in the summers,' she said. 'It bears really beautiful pink flowers.'

He looked up at the tree to see whether he could spot any pink flowers.

'You won't see shit right now dodo,' she laughed mischievously. 'You know, I thought of something funny the other day...' she continued.

'What's that?' he asked.

'I realized how much I miss high school.'

'You hated high school. I can understand if you said junior college but high school...really? I can barely remember it...It's just a haze for me.'

'That's why I miss it, I think,' she said.

She passed the cigarette back to Rehan as he processed the thought of blurry objects holding the most allure. He inhaled and let the smoke out, watching it swirl.

They sat in silence looking at each other, both entranced by the twinkle in each other's eyes.

Rehan sighed and took another drag.

'These are some of the best moments of my life,' said Sasha.

'Really?'

'I can just relax out here. You know?' she said.

'Yeah I know...I know.'

In the distance, laughter and footsteps could be heard. The two of them paused and sat in attention as four young men climbed up over the fence and walked into the park. They looked like they were in their late teens. One of the boys stuck a key into the side of the floodlight and the park was instantly illuminated.

The four of them froze when they saw Rehan and Sasha sitting there, stock-still and wide-eyed. One of them stepped forward and smiled.

'Hey, I hope I am not disturbing anyone over there?' he said.

'Oh, no, we were about to leave,' said Sasha.

'Well, hey, look you all don't have to go. We were just about play some football, if you want to join...' said another boy.

'Yeah, we could use some extra players,' the first boy added.

'No, really, no...But thank you,' said Rehan.

He took Sasha's hand and started walking away only to slow down a couple of moments later. He stopped and looked at her. She looked back at him, all confused. He turned around and saw the four of them dribbling with the ball. He yelled out to them.

'Hey, you sure we can play?'

❚❚❚

The six of them had a gala time as they played in the rain. Water was splashed, smiles were exchanged, goals scored. To Rehan it felt like he was living his life in school all over again. He looked at Sasha and the way she was smiling and playing enthusiastically made him believe that she felt the same way. Such clarity of mind was rarely available to him and the peace it brought made him ecstatic.

He received the ball and dribbled towards the opposition's goal; skipping past challenges before Sasha drove into him with a nasty tackle that would have earned her a red card at least, shoulder butting him in the chest. He lost his footing and fell down on the ground. The puddles of water in the grass made Sasha slip as well and she landed on top of him. He felt her head smack against his shoulder, the soft press of her breasts on his chest and there was no room for further observation. Strands of her wet hair fell down to cover his face as he looked up into her hazel eyes. He could feel her slow deep breaths on his neck and her hands gently moving on his shoulders trying to regain balance. He knew this feeling; he knew it far too well. Ten years ago he had experienced the exact same thing; the same closeness to her, the same fleeting distance. Back then, he had decided to withdraw himself from it, but today, he felt differently. Today he wanted to cover that iota of distance and kiss her and hold her forever in that lush greenness that surrounded him.

The hortatory whistling from the guys surrounding them broke the spell. Sasha scurried herself back to her feet and brushed her hair back as she looked at the ground uneasily. Rehan hadn't always been a good reader of the subtle innuendoes but he had read it perfectly this time.

'Well, we will make a move now guys,' he said as he stood back up. 'Thanks a lot for letting us play.'

'Anytime man,' said the boy. 'Good night to the two of you.'

❚❚❚

Sasha leaned against the door of her house as Rehan stood against the opposite wall in the porch. Neither one of them had said a word on their way back. Both of them were perhaps just waiting for the other to say something to break the ice. They merely stood there silently and stared at each other. Finally Rehan smiled at her and she smiled back.

'Are you doing anything tomorrow?' he asked her.

Sasha was still smiling.

'Not yet,' she said. 'What do you have planned for tomorrow?'

'I don't know…paintball maybe.'

Sasha nodded and grinned. 'Sounds like a plan,' she said and kissed him on the cheek. She opened the door so that only she could go in. Halfway in the door, she paused and turned around.

'Call me tomorrow?'

'Yeah, I will,' said Rehan.

❚❚❚

Rehan had called Arif to pick him up midway. He had no clue as to why he had done that. Perhaps he wanted someone he could talk to or it could have been the fact that he had no energy left after a long day's trachle. Whatever was the case, he was more than happy to hitch a free ride back home. Arif was waiting for him outside the Chembur station. As soon as Rehan got into the passenger seat and shut the door, the car started moving.

'So you didn't do the deed?' Arif asked him.

'What deed?'

'Don't be a smartass with me,' Arif said.

'What deed?' asked Rehan, perplexed.

'Sex, fuck, make love, stick your penis in her vagina. Still want me to clarify?' said Arif.

Rehan merely continued to watch out of the window, the scenery whizzing him by.

'It's not how you would think,' he said.

'Well then fucking surprise me,' said Arif. 'You know I went to college, I might be smarter than you think.'

'You registered for a diploma in performing arts and failed to attend a single class.'

Arif simply smiled and gave a small shrug. Rehan adjusted himself in his seat and stared back out of the window.

'You know, you have been with that bitch for three days. Has she changed her mind yet?' asked Arif.

'Yeah, she's just about getting there, probably.'

'Well, that's good then,' said Arif. 'So tell me how did the rest of the date go?'

'It went pretty well. You know, I am thinking about getting myself a car.'

'Wow! Great; it's about time,' said Arif.

'Yeah, I think so too. All this travelling lately has got me thinking about it and I think I should finally get one. The trains are too crowded.'

'Yes man, you should. So what are we talking about here? What kind of a car do you want?'

Rehan scratched his stubble ruminating for a while. 'My dad used to own a Mahindra pick-up truck when I was young,' he said. 'You think I could get one of those? Preferably, an older model.'

'Really, a pick-up truck? After all these years you decide to buy a car and you want to buy a shitty pick-up truck. What the fuck is wrong with you man?'

'What? I liked that pick-up truck. You can just park it anywhere and go and lie down in the back and relax, look at the stars and all that,' said Rehan.

'Oh, so that is what you do on your dates with her…look at the stars and all that,' said Arif. 'Anyway, I think the model has changed quite a bit in the times. Your best shot will be getting a second hand one.'

'Yeah, I thought so too. Do you know any guys who deal with all this?' asked Rehan.

'I do actually. His name is Manish, operates out of Mohammed Ali Road next to Zakaria Masjid bus stop.'

'Well, can you hook me up with him sometime?'

'I will do you one better, my friend. I am going to call him up right now,' said Arif.

'Right now? It's fucking eleven thirty at night man,' Rehan said looking at his watch.

'Dude have you never been to Mohammad Ali Road? Nothing shuts down over there until like two at night. Relax…I am just glad that finally you are buying a car. Now I don't have to come pick you up every time. Really am a selfish bastard, am I not?' he teased.

Arif picked up his cell phone and asked Rehan to open his contacts and dial Manish Motors as they cruised past King's Circle on a relatively empty street. Rehan did the needful and handed the cell back to Arif.

'*As-salam alaykum* Manish *Bhai,*' Arif greeted as his call was received. 'How are you?' He waited for a response and then continued, 'Well, I have a friend who is in need of a car…a Mahindra pick-up truck to be specific. Do you have any available?'

He nodded his head while listening intricately and then turned to Rehan.

'He has a 2005 model available in white. He says that it works great and has travelled fifty thousand kilometres. Will be available for two lakhs with registration.'

'Sounds good…when can I have it?' asked Rehan.

'Hey, don't you want to have a look at it first…take a test drive maybe.'

'No, that's fine. Just ask him how soon can I have it and if they accept cheques,' said Rehan.

Arif relayed the questions through his phone.

'He says you can have it tomorrow itself and a cheque will be fine. He is also ready to deliver the car at your place.'

'That's fantastic…ask him to seal the deal,' said Rehan.

Arif did just that. 'I will text you the address of delivery, Manish *bhai*. Goodnight' he said before hanging up.

'Thanks a lot. I owe you one,' said Rehan as he shook Arif's hand.

'No problem man. Hope you take me out on a drive soon. I too want to look at the stars and all that,' Joked Arif, then added, 'Here, type in your address and send it to him.'

Rehan giggled as he looked at him. 'Fucking bastard,' he said taking the cell phone before turning away and staring out of the window.

The car rolled down a silent road before stopping a few blocks away from Rehan's apartment. He stepped out of the car and stood there for a moment as Arif drove away. There was an ATM right behind him. Rehan went inside. After inserting the card and punching in his security pin he made a quick balance enquiry. He waited for his request to be processed. Finally the screen came back to life. It read…

Your Current account balance is – 89, 54,360 Rupees.

Wow, that is a lot of money, Rehan thought. His savings had matured. He could do loads of things with that kind of money. He knew he had another twenty lakhs in his apartment from his recent assignments. He could actually give up his job and run away and start with a clean slate. Rehan walked out of the ATM and back onto the street. He pulled out a cigarette and looked at it, casually running it through his fingers; still contemplating about the life he was living and the one he wanted. Then he finally lit it with a metallic click of his lighter, the magical sparks bringing a flame to life as the tip burned with a bright luminescent red glow. After taking a couple of drags from it, he walked back towards his apartment mulling over such thoughts.

An airplane flew across the overcast sky on a gloomy day, so low that he could feel the vibration of its engines in his bones. He found himself standing in a lush green meadow observing the butterflies as they flitted over the grass. Surrounded by endless acres of land with trees and flowers and butterflies, he felt more peaceful than he had ever felt. Far across at a distance he saw her, covered in a majestic purple halter neck dress walking on the sward. He could swear on his life that she was the most beautiful girl he had ever seen almost as if she had an aura of brilliance about her. He started walking towards her slowly at first and then gathering pace, finally breaking into a dash. The ringing of a bell could be heard across the skies. It did not sound like a church bell to him. The bell rang again and suddenly his vision started blurring. He could no longer spot her. The sky had turned black and the meadow had become a swamp. The ringing of the bell intensified and he found himself sinking in the swamp until everything turned dark and he could not see anything.

Rehan found himself lying in his bed with his hair askew and eyes refusing to open. The sun had risen and it looked like a clear day. He heard the ringing again, it was his door bell.

Some way to ruin a perfect dream, he thought and finally got out of the covers. He pulled on a vest and answered the door.

'Rehan Irani?' asked the man at the door.

'Yes.'

'Sir, we have come to deliver your car,' said the man. 'Would you like to take a drive and see if you are satisfied with it?'

'Actually I just woke up,' said Rehan, 'but it's okay...I trust you guys. Just wait here and I will hand you the cheque.'

Rehan had the cheque prepared and he grabbed it from a drawer in his wardrobe. He handed it to the man, took possession of the keys and sent the man on his way.

'We have parked the car right outside the building, it's a white pickup. The papers are in the glove box,' said the man before leaving.

The clock in his living room showed the time - 10:25 a.m. Rehan went out into his balcony and saw his purchase standing right below him. Just seeing that white pick-up truck instilled him with some unusual energy. He picked up his phone and scrolled through his contacts name by name before reaching Sasha. His finger slid along the green call button, lingering on it for a while. Suddenly he hit cancel and looked at the time. It was 10:35 a.m. Rehan sighed and pulled out a cigarette, and lit it.

Five minutes later, the cigarette was gone and only the filter remained in his hand. Rehan tossed it over the balcony and took out his phone. He couldn't wait any longer. God! So stymied was he by her thoughts. He called her and she picked it up after three rings.

'This is the earliest yet,' she said laughing.

'I...I...' Rehan stuttered, taken aback by her greeting, but recovered quickly. 'I just bought a new car...I mean actually it's an old car but I just bought it so I wanted to know if you wanted to meet up, or something.'

He could hear her giggle on the other side of the line.

'Alright, where?' she asked.

◖◗◖◗◖◗

A regular one hour drive had turned into two. The traffic had been bad and Rehan detested it totally. All along the way he had contemplated whether buying a car had been a wise idea. But now as he sat next to Sasha in the park near her place, he couldn't care less about it. Whenever she looked at him, he forgot about almost everything that was bothering him. In her presence he felt at ease; he felt tranquil and inspired.

'So if you could go anywhere in the world, anywhere, where would it be?' Sasha asked him.

'You mean other than Essel World?'

Sasha chuckled, but quickly straightened up. She urged him to give a straight answer.

'I've always wanted to go to Paris. To warp the words of Gretrude Stein—India is my country and Paris is my hometown,' he said.

'Same,' she said and continued. 'Have you ever been out of the country?'

'Yeah, once.'

'Where?'

'Andaman,' said Rehan.

Sasha laughed at his joke and looked up at him beaming. 'FYI, that's still in the country.'

He chuckled, 'I know. And apologies, I bring you here a lot, but I don't really know where else to go.'

'Well, I love this park anyway,' said Sasha as she peered into his eyes. 'It's really pretty. I feel alive here.'

Rehan nodded as he reached into his pocket and fingered a pack of cigarettes. He started pulling it out but paused and scanned Sasha, who was in a trance with the undulating pond. He slid the cigarette back into his pocket and released a heavy breath.

'What's the funniest story you know?' she asked him.

'Oh, wow...oh so many,' he said surprised at the randomness of her question.

'Really?'

'I'm not much of a story guy,' said Rehan.

'So you don't have many?'

'Oh, I've got stories,' he said a little taken aback. 'I'm just not a good storyteller.'

'Try one,' she said.

Rehan glared out over the pond, incredulously, his face creasing in concentration. Finally, he took a deep breath.

'A funny one?'

'Yeah.'

He shook his head in disbelief and scratched his hair. 'Alright, I got one,' he said and narrated. 'So this one time, I and my friend Arif were driving back from Lonavala at about two in the morning. It was really fucking dark outside... obviously.'

He glanced at her and she urged him to continue. A smile spread across her face.

'And then, in the distance we saw three hitchhikers, it was dark and we couldn't really make them out...So we pulled over and all of a sudden I see two white eyes and a deep, deep voice.' Rehan lowered his voice and continued in a deep baritone. 'Where you heading? And before we could reply, three big black men got inside our car.'

Sasha giggled at this.

'They were about 6'3" and heavily built. So we got a little nervous, naturally...Ends up they were some Nigerian football players who had missed the bus, due to a little partying and a visit to a friend's place trying to get to Mumbai.'

Sasha laughed and rested her head on his shoulder.

'Ended up being some of the nicest guys we ever picked up,' he said.

'That was a pretty funny story,' she said. 'See you're not a horrible storyteller.'

Rehan merely shrugged, knowing she said that to just please him and pulled out a cigarette, he lit it and stared ahead.

'Yeah, funny story,' he said glancing over the panorama of the park. Some children were floating paper boats in the distance. A couple walked their dog while chatting. Rehan looked at Sasha.

'Let's go someplace else,' he said.

███

Rehan and Sasha walked through the crowded Inorbit Mall, lost in the clutter as people rushed around them. Finally pushing their way through the sea of people, they reached the food court.

'You hungry?' she asked him.

'Not particularly,' he said. 'You?'

'Nope, but we can sit here and rest for a bit.' They had been strolling aimlessly for about an hour.

The roar of the crowd could be heard as they sat facing each other silently.

'Any store in particular you want to go to?' he said breaking the ice.

'You're the one who brought me here, remember,' she said and looked at him absently.

'Well, it's warm and dry in here,' he said and paused before continuing. 'I don't know, I figured I'd buy you anything you want. On me.'

She smiled at the offer and her cheeks turned a little red. 'Thanks, but no thanks,' she said.

'Seriously, we'll go window shopping. Anything you want, on me,' Rehan tried persuasively.

'I...I...really don't want anything,' she stuttered. 'Honestly.'

He looked at her baffled. *Since when did girls start hating shopping?* he thought. His go-to plan was failing miserably.

Sasha stood up abruptly. 'Screw the mall. Let's go somewhere else,' she said, turned around and started walking. Rehan shrugged and followed her to the escalator.

'The reason I don't want anything is not completely because I feel bad taking your money,' she said as they descended down the escalator. 'It's just that I truly believe nothing in here is really going to have an impact on my life.'

There was a lot of hidden pain in her words and Rehan realised it. This version of her made him uncomfortable. For some time now, he had thought the perhaps he was having some effect on her, maybe making her question herself. But when she said words like these; he just couldn't bring himself to see her in the eyes and change the topic. There always were those awkward long moments when neither of them said a word as they zoned out analogously.

'I have to use the bathroom,' he said brightening as they neared the exit. 'Will see you in the car.'

'Sure,' she said catching a hint of something amiss but made her way to the parking lot.

Rehan entered a cubicle in the washroom and immediately called Arif.

'Hello?' came the answer.

'Arif, Rehan here,' he said. 'Have you guys had dinner yet?'

'No. Why?'

'You and Priya should come to dinner with me and Sasha,' Rehan said.

'That sounds good. Where do you want to go?'

'Jazz by the Bay in a couple of hours?'

'Cool, we shall see you there,' Arif said and hung up.

Sasha saw Rehan walking towards the car through a frosted window. He got in the car and said...

'So, my friends Arif and Priya invited us to go to dinner with them tonight. Do you mind?'

▌▌▌

The band played the '60s classic song 'Nobody knows the trouble I have seen' by Louis Armstrong in the restaurant as Rehan and Sasha sat in a booth near the window overlooking Marine Drive. Silence washed over them for a few moments before Rehan grinned and waved looking towards the entrance. Arif walked in with his wife Priya, a woman in her early thirties. She was short and fair, a little chubby, with a cute face and visibly pregnant. The four of them greeted and shook hands from afar before getting situated in the booth except Rehan and Arif who hugged each other as Arif whispered, 'You owe me one brother. This took a lot of persuasion.'

'Well, you look better than the first time I saw you,' Arif told Sasha. Priya laughed and Rehan let out a nervous chuckle.

Sasha blushed but quickly regained her composure with a smile. 'So how long have you two been married?' she asked.

'Two happy years now,' said Priya.

Arif winked at Rehan and raised his beer glass high. All of them toasted and drank. The conversation began and not for a moment did Sasha ever feel left out of the group. Arif and Priya had been extremely warm to her and for the first time in many days, she felt like she belonged somewhere. As they laughed and drank together no one could have said that they were all meeting for the first time. For everyone else it seemed as if they were a close knit group having a gala time. As the waitress returned and placed their food on the table, Priya took a huge chug from her drink.

'Careful, sweetheart! Remember we have a baby in your tummy,' said Arif.

'Oh, shut up!' Priya retorted loudly and obnoxiously.

Sasha turned towards Rehan, reached under the table and grabbed his hand. His face lit up.

The music slowly faded away and there was a round of applause for the musicians. They announced that they would be taking a break for some time and made their way off the stage.

'Dude, why don't you go and play something,' Arif told Rehan. 'I have never heard you play.'

'Are you crazy? We are in a restaurant with a hell lot of people... I don't know...' Rehan said.

'So what? I am sure you can handle it.' Arif turned to the ladies and continued, 'Do you know that he plays the trumpet like a maestro?'

'Saxophone,' Rehan corrected.

'Ya, ya, same shit. Now just play already.'

'Yes Rehan, you should! Even I want to hear you play,' Priya chipped in.

Rehan felt his hand being squeezed. He turned to see Sasha smiling at him.

'Please play,' she mumbled sweetly.

'Okay fine,' he said and made his way towards the stage. No way could he refuse that voice anything. He caught hold of the restaurant manager and explained his friend's plea to him. The manager too did not take much convincing and quickly went up to the stage and made the announcement public. There was no backing out now.

For years now Rehan had played the instrument in his solitude and the confinements of his house. Never had a thought of a public performance ever crossed his mind. It was not that he had stage fright, but for him playing the saxophone had always been a thing for his own leisure. Today, as he stepped out on that stage, he was getting rid of his carapace. His inhibitions were wearing away. He picked up the instrument and brought it close to his mouth. And with one deep breath all his dubiety vanished. He started playing the tune of Alone by Kenny G, hitting every chord perfectly, capturing the audience with the harmony, making love to the instrument like he always did; he played the tune to a tee and when it was over he opened his eyes to a room of thunderous applause. It was like nothing he had ever experienced before; the attention, the enormous love and appreciation, it made Rehan feel good about himself. He turned around to quickly look at Sasha and his friends. They too seemed to be completely mesmerized by his performance and were applauding him proudly.

After bowing down elegantly to his audience, Rehan made his way back to his table with a wide smile on his face.

'Man, that was fantastic,' said Arif. 'I had no idea you could play this well.'

'Thanks.'

'No, I am serious. That was amazing, wasn't it?' He asked the ladies who nodded in approval. 'I am definitely going to try listening to things other than Hip Hop.'

'Oh ya! Rehan told me about your Hip Hop saga,' Sasha said. 'What is up with that?'

'Well nothing is up with that,' responded Priya before Arif could even begin. 'He wanted to be a rapper and fell flat on his face. Thank god I walked into his life or else god knows where he would have been.'

'Baby, don't go around crushing my feelings. I too have hopes and ambitions,' said Arif sarcastically.

'Had!' Priya corrected.

'So do you have any fun stories to tell from your experiences?' Sasha asked him.

'Ya dude, tell us a funny story. She loves stories and you know how bad I am at them,' Rehan added.

'All right, fine...one of the craziest things that happened to me was...well...' Arif began

'Before you go on, try and keep it clean,' Rehan interrupted.

'Well, fuck,' Arif said.

Rehan rolled his eyes and looked at Sasha. She laughed along with Priya.

'Alright, alright, I'll try and keep it U/A,' said Arif.

'Keep going!' Sasha encouraged him.

'Fine, damn...well, there are some images that stay with you forever.' Arif went on.

It was a festive atmosphere and everyone listened to him intently; laughing and exclaiming at his maliciously hilarious tale about being hit on by a homosexual music composer; his enthusiasm was contagious and exciting. Everyone enjoyed his energetic and passionate storytelling.

'He only said fuck three times without noticing,' said Rehan after Arif had finished telling his story.

'Wow, that was really messed up,' added Sasha through her laughter.

'And that was only the U/A version. Guess what the alternate ending in the A version was,' Rehan joked.

'Fuck you,' quipped Arif.

Everyone laughed, evidently at ease. The music continued playing as they kept talking and smiling into the wee hours of the night.

▌▐ ▌

Rehan and Sasha came out of the restaurant as Arif and Priya followed. The night was clear and a cool breeze blew across Marine Drive. It had been a good day, at least Rehan felt so. He knew that Sasha had a good time and that was the sole purpose anyway. They waved Arif and Priya goodbye and headed towards the car. After backing the car out of the parking lot, Rehan drove down a fantastically illuminated road.

Sasha looked out of the window sitting in the passenger seat while Rehan stared out towards the road.

'That was fun,' she said slicing the silence.

'Yeah, yeah... it was a lot of fun.'

'Nice guy,' she added.

'Yeah, he's quite a laugh. He's been my support system for quite a while.'

That awkward silence returned as Sasha gazed out at the oncoming traffic and as always it made Rehan uneasy.

'Pretty good food, huh?' he tried making small talk.

Sasha nodded and continued to look out the window.

'You want to come back to my place?' he asked almost instinctively.

She gave him another nod and leaned her head back against the rest.

❚ ❚ ❚

Sasha sat on the couch in Rehan's apartment while he prepared some coffee in the kitchen. She looked around the living room; it was just like her house, her life: barren. Rehan came out of the kitchen holding two mugs of coffee. She gave him the best smile that she could muster. He handed her a mug and went over to an empty chair on the opposite side of the hall.

'Want to watch some TV?' he asked.

Sasha took a sip of her coffee and then placed the mug on the centre table. She got up from the couch, walked up to Rehan and planted a kiss on cheek. She whispered something seductively into his ear and then looked right into his eyes. He was rendered speechless for a moment and then a smile crept up on his face.

'I'm not doing all this just to sleep with you,' he said.

'I know, that's why I want you to,' she replied.

Rehan chuckled briefly and shook his head avoiding eye contact.

'What's so funny?' asked Sasha.

'Well this feels exactly like it was ten years ago,' he said. 'You know, the night of our farewell.'

'Ya, it does…I suppose.'

'But you know what's really funny? I have thought about that night like a million times over the years. Thinking that maybe I could have done things differently.'

'Well life has given you a second chance at it again,' she said. 'That really doesn't happen that often, you know.'

'Ya, I know. But I think I am going to pass…again,' said Rehan and started walking off towards the balcony.

Sasha looked at his departing figure in disbelief. She felt stupid and cheap.

'Why?' she almost screamed. 'Don't you like me?'

He stopped at the entrance of the balcony and turned around to face her.

'Of course I like you,' he said. 'Hell, like would be a major understatement there. But this is not the way I want things to go down between us. Not when I am not sure whether your death wish is more important or I am. I wish this to be something without dark clouds on the horizon.' And he did. Impermanence after he committed himself would kill him surely. He needed to be sure; he needed her to be sure.

Sasha found herself at a loss of words. There was an obvious tension in the air. Both of them sensed it. Rehan decided to walk away and stepped out into the balcony. He stared out at the open sky and at the stars overhead. A few minutes later she walked in and stood next to him. The plaintive silence made them both awkward and yet it gave them the time to understand each other.

'It's really peaceful out here,' she said, finally breaking it.

'Yeah, it is,' he replied.

Sasha took a deep breath and continued.

'Do you ever feel like maybe, if things went differently when you were younger, certain situations avoided, you'd somehow turn out a more complete human being?'

Rehan was in awe as he looked out at the stars. Sasha always managed to surprise him with her words. He slowly gazed down at her. He held her hand tightly and looked into her eyes.

'A man is complete only in death,' he said contemplatively. A naughty smile crept up on his face as he continued, 'But different, yes. No shit!' kissing her gently on her eyelids. God! He loved the tiny capillaries crisscrossing those delicate features. He loved the way they fluttered in expectation, how her pulse raced under his fingers. She was alive, and so was he. That was all that mattered.

13th June 2013

It was unusually cold for a June morning. The chill in the air was made more evident by the grey billowing clouds that filled the sky till the horizon. Rehan sat inside the Vista Café in The Taj Land's End Hotel with a newspaper on his table. Looking out at the violent sea and seeing the waves crash against the shore made him feel irritable. He couldn't single out a reason for his peevishness among the millions that made his everyday life hell; but something about this day just did not feel right. He turned his attention back at the newspaper and went over the front page news. Utter garbage as usual. Public media was starting to repel him; even on the TV, he could stand nothing more than Animal Planet and the like. So much simpler, their rules of life.

'Hi, I am Riya,' the waitress came up from behind and startled Rehan. 'I am going to be your server today. Can I get you something to start out with?' she asked.

'Nope, I am waiting for one more, thanks,' he said.

'Ok, well you sure you don't need water or something to drink?'

'Oh, no thanks, I'll uh...wait for her,' said Rehan.

'Should have known you would be with a lady,' she quipped.

The door of the Cafe opened and Sasha walked in wearing a grey sweat shirt and track pants, hair pulled in a tight pony tail; quite unlike her. She stood in the doorway and scanned the coffee shop until she finally spotted Rehan. She made her way towards him. Riya walked up to her and greeted her kindly.

'And here we are! I'll give you two a minute,' she said as Sasha approached the table. Her eyes seemed puffy on a close look.

Rehan stood up to greet her. He smiled a little, but only at the corner of his lips.

'Hey, how are you?' he asked her.

'Good, but I couldn't sleep last night,' said Sasha.

'Why?'

'I had a weird dream.'

'Huh. Good thing it was only a dream because mine are no better,' said Rehan as he picked up the menu and began scanning it quietly.

Sasha merely stared at him from across the table.

'You don't want to know about my dream?' she asked.

'Are you interested in telling me?' he said and looked up at her.

'Well, not anymore,' she said, looking miffed.

'But you wanted to talk about it?' Rehan asked.

'I guess so.'

'So, let me hear it.'

Sasha sighed and reclined against the cushion. Rehan leaned forward in response, looking at her intently.

'It sounds stupid now,' she said, 'running it back through my head. I don't know.'

'Come one, tell me. I want to know,' he said uncomfortably.

'It's stupid thinking about it.'

'Okay, fine...tell me when you're ready,' said Rehan.

'Well...I mean...,' she trailed into thought.

'Look, tell me the fucking story or don't tell me...shit!' He said, immediately regretting his outburst. This was not the way he wanted to go but man, was she testing his patience.

Riya entered as if right on cue. She maintained a real smile this time, obviously having overheard the conversation.

'Hello! Have you decided what I can start you off with?' she asked.

'Umm...could you give us two more minutes?' Rehan requested

'Certainly.'

'Thanks, Riya.'

Riya went over to the next table and began picking up the cutlery and plates. Rehan turned to Sasha and leaned in again.

'Friendly with her, aren't you?' she teased.

'Friendlier with you girl, do you know what you want to get?' he asked her.

'Yeah, I want the oriental breakfast,' she said.

'I think I'm just going to get pancakes.'

'Huh, don't I feel like the fat ass,' Sasha said angrily.

'No, of course not, you look...pretty,' said Rehan as he was caught off guard.

The awkward silence took over. Sasha looked down at her lap briefly and then back up at Rehan.

'Specially with the *gulaabi ankhein* effect going on here,' he said, in an attempt to laugh it off.

'Hilarious!' she laughed as they gazed at each other.

The moment was broken by him as he turned around...

'Riya, I think we're ready to order.'

❚❚❚

Colonel Puri sat inside his office overlooking the city on the forty-first floor of the Pegasus Estate. Another man sat on the chair across the table. His hands moved fervently as his hollow eyes frantically scanned the Colonel. Dressed up in plain blue shirt and faded denims, he looked like he was in his mid-thirties. The Rolex on his left wrist and the platinum bracelet on his right were suggestive of his affluent lifestyle.

'Choosing to die, well, it's your god given right,' said Colonel Puri. But inside, he was always disgusted by such people. Too weak to live and too weak to die. God's chosen scum who couldn't appreciate what was given and would now die like vermin.

The man in the chair didn't speak, nor did he even look at the Colonel.

'Free will, well that's something that comes with a burden, son,' Puri continued. 'A major burden. The choices we make in life lead us down different paths. Correct?'

The man continued to look down, twitching at random intervals.

'Mr Shinde, am I correct?' Colonel Puri asked again.

'Yes,' said the man.

The Colonel peered deep into his eyes. He could see his fear and hesitation. Mister Sagar Shinde was in two minds about this and that was something which the Colonel did not want on his conscience.

'Listen, Sagar. This isn't a game, you know that,' said the Colonel. 'People have the right to die. If the pain in this world is too strong, why not pass on? Let go of the pain. Free will means a lot of things, to suck it up and live or to succumb and die in search of better havens. Your call.'

A brief moment of silence intervened before the man spoke.

'I want to die,' he said.

'Okay then. Two fifteen a.m. at your house. Until then you can take care of the payment procedure.'

The man turned around and started walking towards the door when the Colonel called out to him...

'Oh and Sagar!'

'Yes?'

'You sure? Because once you walk out of those doors, you can't change your mind.' The Colonel asked for one final confirmation.

Mister Shinde showed no facial expression, he walked to the door, opened it and then slammed it violently as he left.

I guess he's sure Colonel Puri thought.

❚❚❚

At the Vista Café, Rehan and Sasha had finished half of their breakfast. Sasha took a bite of her dim sum and looked at Rehan. A smile crept up on her face.

'Hey, remember cultural night?' she asked. 'Do you remember what I wore?'

'I didn't go to cultural night with you,' he said.

'I know, but do you remember?'

'I know you're hoping for a romantic answer,' he said. 'But I was busy on the backside of the auditorium, bumming around with the guys.'

'Why?'

'Because cultural night was the most boring night in school. And I had no interest in watching that Shweta girl and her theatre group performing some stupid play,' said Rehan.

'Well, that's fairly rude. She was a good friend of mine, and I was wearing a purple dress.'

'Huh, actually, that I vaguely remember.' He didn't remember his dress, but her's, well...Prime difference between men and women.

Rehan took a bite of his pancakes. He smiled at her but she merely stared back coldly.

He began to ask, 'Wha..' but was cut short by his cell phone as it buzzed to life on the table. He looked down and saw the screen flash - Arif calling.

'I have to get this.' He said and answered the phone. 'Hello?'

'Rehan, we are meeting the boss at four thirty,' said Arif.

'What? I thought we had the week off?'

'Well, apparently not,' said Arif and hung up.

Rehan placed the phone on the table and looked at Sasha. She glared at him.

'So who was that?' she asked.

'I got to meet my boss at four thirty,' he said. 'No biggie, it shouldn't take more than an hour, promise.'

Rehan smiled at her. She turned away to look out the window at the cold June morning.

'Am I a special case, or has this happened before?' she asked still looking out.

Rehan was taken aback. It took him a moment to straighten up in his seat and look back at her.

'What?'

'Am I a special case, or have you tried to save all of your clients?' Sasha yawped bluntly.

'You are a special case... Of course, you are! If some random dude decides to kill himself, what can I do to stop him? With you, I could at least try,' Rehan said. There was an evident hesitation in his voice. He took a bite of his pancake and allowed the silence to fill up between them. Sasha continued to stare coldly out of the window.

Rehan realized this and put his fork and knife down opposite her. Finally he cleared his throat.

'Something wrong, Sasha?' he asked.

She didn't break her gaze from the outside world as she spoke, it was clear that a tear fell from her eye.

'You know you killed my father... Some random dude, right?'

Rehan stared at her incredulously. His eyebrows creased and he let out a heavy sigh. He leaned in and reached for her hand. She immediately pulled it back.

'I never knew that was your father,' he said. 'Had I known, I would never have...killed him.'

She closed her eyes and a new, fresh set of tears spilled down her face.

'I promise you, I didn't know,' he continued.

'Why do you do this Rehan?' she asked. 'Why did you choose this job?'

Rehan allowed himself a brief second as he took a large deep breath and started to turn his coffee mug in circles. He slowly lifted his head to make eye contact with her. His shoulders hunched forward as he steadied himself before narrating his story.

▮▮▮

Rehan and Arif sat across Colonel Puri in his study as he gazed at them intently. The clock on the wall showed the time as four thirty.

'You guys got another one tonight,' he said.

'I thought we had the week off?' Rehan quizzed.

'You did. You got four days off, didn't you, you lazy bum,' said the Colonel.

'That's not a week,' said Arif.

'Anyway, I will text you the details of the hit in the evening. The target stays in the penthouse of a building in Dadar, so expect security to be high. Keep your silencers on for this one,' The Colonel concluded.

'Anything else?' asked Rehan.

'No. You can leave,' said Puri. 'I want Arif to stay back for a couple of minutes. Need to discuss some family matters.'

'Ya, sure,' said Rehan. 'I will wait for you in your car,' he told Arif.

'Why?' asked the Colonel.

'Because he will drop me home.'

'Haven't you got your car?' asked Arif.

'No dude, there was some waterlogging in Mahim so I left it there and took the train,' said Rehan. He was a little bemused by their intrigue about his vehicle. 'Why, is there a problem?'

The Colonel waved his hand at him, 'No, you go ahead. I will send Arif down in just a few minutes.'

'Fine.'

Rehan made his way out of the study and shut the door behind him. The Colonel could hear his footsteps as he descended the stairs. Convinced that Rehan was gone, he turned around to face Arif who was looking at him.

'What it is boss?' he asked.

'Listen to me because this is very important.' The Colonel began. 'You are like a son to me and someday I want you to take over our business. But for that to happen, we need to eliminate someone.'

'Who?' asked Arif.

'I will send you a text before your assignment tonight. That will be your next assignment. And you have to complete it tonight itself.' The Colonel ran his palm over his face and took a deep breath. He then looked back at Arif who still had his focus intact. 'Now it is very important for you to understand that this second target does not fit your job description, nor does it fall in the company's assignment protocol. But for Greener Pasture's functionality, he has to be eliminated. Get it?'

'I do,' said Arif.

'I know it's outside your line of duty, so be sure before you agree. You must not fail tonight, Arif. Our future might depend on this,' said the Colonel.

'Don't worry boss. You just give me the details. I will take care of the rest.'

'Very well then. You may leave now,' the Colonel waved him to the door.

Arif got up from his seat and made his way towards the exit when the Colonel called out to him again.

'Oh and Arif...don't mention any of this to Rehan right now. You know how he is. His morals might make him overreact, and I don't want two botched assignments.'

'Sure sir,' Arif said and trotted out.

As the door closed, the Colonel sank back in his chair as if deep in thought. He had given it due consideration and there could be no other way. He wasn't the ruthless cold blooded killer he appeared to be, but then some loose ends just needed to be tied. Loose ends... he thought, looking up at the portrait over the fireplace.

Vikram… you were no loose end. Why then did you have to go? He could still see him in his memories as if it were yesterday. Intelligent eyes, ruffled hair and a tiny nose. The Colonel smiled. *God can't have too fair creatures roam this earth, I suppose.* At such a young age, such a tragic disease had wasted him until all the brightness had left his eyes. Frail and weak in the third stage of leukaemia when it had all but eaten away his mind, Vikram could no longer recognize anyone, nor speak coherently. His mother could no longer bear to look at him and hence avoided him completely. All attempts had failed and the chemo was only making it worse. The Colonel had to understand that there was no use banging on the door that wasn't about to open. He couldn't let it rot and the only thing left was to burn it.

Such a peaceful morning it was when he took Vikram's hand in his. He was still in military service then and had a huge sprawling bungalow in Shimla bordering the woods. It broke his heart into a million shards to look into his son's eyes that had no sense of emotion; only a weary pain. He knew then what he had to do…

The cold metal of his 0.90 Caliber Baretta felt cold in his waistband, almost as cold as his heart as he led his son out, half walking him, half carrying, he took him to a stream a few miles down a rugged forest lane; caressed his cheek, ruffled his hair as he pointed the gun to his son's head. Even then, there was no response from Vikram, like always. He couldn't comprehend what it all meant, but just looked blankly at this sobbing person who was his father. One clean shot in the head, tears blinding the Colonel all the while he dug the grave in the soft earth by the brook with his bare hands and buried him there. Didn't even need a big hole, considering the barely 35 kg body.

He quit the service the next day, left for Mumbai with his wife to live with his sister who worked in a pharmacy then. Since then, he had vowed to let every person choose his or her death and to help them along in the process. He had the necessary tradecraft to undertake his course and he set on it, never looking back ever since.

He couldn't let anyone mar the legacy his son had left in his heart. He wouldn't let anybody ruin his life's hardest work.

▌ ▌

Rehan sat in the passenger seat of Arif's car, expressionless as he looked out of the window and watched the scenery fly by. The sky was still overcast and a strong zephyr imparted an unusual iciness to the air. Arif abruptly pulled the car over in a parking spot.

'Why are you stopping?' asked Rehan.

'Something's wrong man,' said Arif.

'With what?'

'Your sorry ass,' he said as he leaned back in the car shrugged and locked all the doors.

'Nothing is wrong man. It's just something about this day,' said Rehan.

'Don't lie to me.'

'I am not lying. And you are going to take me hostage or what?'

'If that is what it takes?' said Arif.

Rehan perspired heavily and leaned back too... 'Well, since I'm going to be here for a while...' he said and pulled out a cigarette and a lighter.

Arif's eyes became wide in fear.

'Hey, motherfucker, you better not. Priya will be pissed.'

Rehan proceeded to light it and took a long drag. He allowed a waft of smoke to come out from his mouth and fill the car.

'Fine! Fuck you, get out,' said Arif and unlocked the door. Rehan climbed out, turned and waved back at Arif, who drove off.

The hustle bustle of the city awaited Rehan. It had been ages since he had walked these streets last. The pace of everything which surrounded him thrilled him today and walking those two miles back home did not seem like a bad idea now. He allowed the vista of the city to sink in before he started walking.

The street market of this city had always been very special. Rehan wondered why he did not come here that often. All afternoon he had been gloomy and irritable but the energy around him was really livening up his spirits.

A man, presumably in his late fifties, stood behind a booth of bananas and grapes. As he saw Rehan approaching he said...

'Have you ever tried real grapes?'

A smile appeared on Rehan's face. 'As opposed to fake grapes?' he asked him.

'Funny guy! Try one of these grapes and tell me what the world has to offer,' said the man and gave him a juicy looking bunch.

Rehan took a few grapes, sniffed at them and popped them in his mouth. His head nodded in approval after a second. He gave the man a thumbs-up and bought some.

He walked along the vendors, smiling, talking and just taking it all in with alternate puffs of cigarette smoke and bites of grapes. He liked the opposing flavours. At a distance he saw a stand, almost obscured by a cycle rickshaw where an old man sat. The man looked as if he was in his late sixties. He had a gaunt face with dark cave like eyes and a worn look, as though he had seen too much. He was peeling an orange with a weak smile. Rehan's attention was captured by the ruggedness of his small stand. He walked over, observing the old man, who was selling books of some sort, with simple black covers and the titles in white bold block letters, appearing hand painted. Closer inspection made him realize they were poems.

'So who wrote these poems?' Rehan asked him.

The man greeted him with a large grin. He reached out with his hand and Rehan took it, giving a firm shake.

'Why, I did,' said the man. 'Every poem in there is by me. I wanted to come out on a lovely day and spread my rambling thoughts to fellow earth dwellers. But sadly, the weather took a bad turn and I wish I could say differently of my customers.'

Rehan had never been one for philosophical talks. Mere words of the man sounded like poetry to him.

'The name's Frank. Just Frank,' the man continued.

'Rehan.'

The man gave him a strong smile. Rehan couldn't stop himself as a laugh escaped from his lips.

'What gave you the inspiration to write poems, Frank?' he asked.

'Well, in this world of users, rarely does a creator come by. Thousands listen to music, few know how to play. Thousands read; but few write,' said the man. 'Where are the current day philosophers? There are so many stories around and yet so few who narrate. I have had my own experiences, my own adventures and my own thoughts. I recognize that those things are solely mine, but then what use would they be if my life can't help the lives of others. That's why I started writing poetry, to give the world what it has given me.'

Rehan nodded with a grin on his face which spread from ear-to-ear as he gazed at the Books of Poems.

'OK, how much?' he asked the man.

'It's free,' said Frank.

This man totally bemused Rehan with each word he said as he looked back at him, baffled.

'What? Then why not put up a "free poems" sign? Tons of people would come,' said Rehan.

'It's only free for those who truly want it,' said Frank.

'How would you know?' he asked.

The man gave an enigmatic smile with the words, 'I did know just now, didn't I? Not all methods need be known… Take this one,' as he picked up a book.

Rehan took it from his hand as he nodded at Frank who returned the favour and leaned back to soak up the sun which had just become incipient.

'The weather is changing brother… Hope you are ready,' he said, still looking at the sun.

Rehan took the small book of poems and slipped a hundred rupee note onto the table while Frank was not looking. He turned to leave and managed a few steps as Frank called out to him.

'Fair warning! It's been a tough year. This issue is a little darker than usual.'

▯ ▯ ▯

Rehan emerged into the living room of his apartment carrying a couple of bags which he placed on the kitchen counter. He wandered inside his bedroom and plopped down on his bed, holding the book of poems titled "Frost". He opened it and read one poem randomly selected.

The trees around me sway,
So more droplets may,
On this feeble body, fall.
I know it will be my last day.
Can almost hear him call.
The words sound garbled,
The sights seem blurred.
Why oh why, this endless pit,
Into which I now fall.
'It's too soon!' I shout to the wind,
The only response a peal of laughter,
'A lot yet I have to see.'
Then a whisper as if in my ear,
'That is why son, I am here.'
But oh! The fear,
The urge to escape...
But into what? This was his fate.
My time is up, I surmise,
Better go head held high,
Whether it be life or demise.

His eyes lingered on the page for a few seconds as he ran the poem over again in his head. He picked up his phone and went through it. He stopped at Sasha. After calculating for a second, he looked back out of the window. The story had not quite the effect he hoped for. Instead of understanding, he received pity. And well, considering he had killed her father, he couldn't expect any more. She was already taking it better than he had expected...

🔫🔫🔫

A digital clock on a nightstand blinked 5:30. Sasha lay down on her torn-up couch in her living room, broken down and defeated. Eyes red, body deprived of food, the apartment dark and cluttered. It was dull and depressing mirroring her thoughts. She could see the silhouette of her dad enjoying his life, happy, as he had never been for years. She wanted to be that happy, that carefree as the silhouette turned into the bloody rocking chair of his room. She was in a trance with her cracked ceiling.

After a couple of minutes she slouched over to her table, reached into the drawer and pulled out a tiny roll of polythene, untied the rubber band and carefully unrolled it as if its contents were made of gold.

Slowly lifting some on the edge of her ATM card, she put it on an overturned plastic plate. Her hands shook as she shaped it into three lines. A hundred rupee note lay rolled poised as if frequently used.

A short snort left the trail clean, just like she wanted her life to be.

And then another…

And another…

❚ ❚ ❚

Rehan leaned casually against the wall in his bedroom. He had his phone in his hand as it kept ringing.

'The number you have called…is not responding…,' the speakerphone announced.

Rehan immediately hung up, leaned back and placed the phone next to himself. His eyes wanted to fall asleep desperately, but his mind wouldn't allow that to happen; not unless he spoke to Sasha. He got back to his feet and made his way into the kitchen. After pulling out a beer from his fridge, he sat down on a chair and looked at the clock intensely. It was 7.55 p.m. There wasn't much that he could do but heave and inebriate.

❚ ❚ ❚

Sasha lay on her bed passed out after what seemed like hours of frenzy and thoughtless bliss. Finally she stirred and abruptly sat up as beads of sweat lingered on her forehead. The tactile hallucinations still working as she got out of bed, wearing only her underwear strolled over to the shower and turned it on. The water ran freely for a moment as she watched it, motionless. She got herself into the shower momentarily. The water was freezing. She stepped out instantly; shivering and looking very pale. A strong sense of nausea overtook her as she focused her attention down at the bathroom floor, her insides wringing. Within a few seconds she leaned over, about to vomit, but the empty retches were all that echoed in the small room.

॥॥॥

Two hours and three beers later, Rehan had still not heard from Sasha. He sat on his balcony, cuddled in a blanket against the harsh air. He smoked a cigarette and peered out over the darkness. Cascades of thoughts were buzzing in his head; one more terrifying than the other. From her being run over by a truck to her slitting her wrist, Rehan had contemplated about it all. He took a deep breath and tightened the blanket over himself. An empty mind always tended to be frantic. Classic human tendency, he made himself understand so as to calm himself. But to no avail.

Suddenly, his phone rang; he reached over clumsily, grabbed it and answered immediately.

'Hello?'

'You called...' it was Sasha, her voice sounding gruff but clear; almost bordering on loud.

'Yeah, I...' Rehan began but was interrupted.

'Six times,' she said curtly.

Rehan had been worried sick about her. The sound of her voice felt soothing. He sighed and thick fumes of vapour omitted from his mouth, swirling like smoke in the cold air.

'Yeah, I wanted to see you,' he said glancing at the stars.

A moment of silence followed as Rehan watched his breath in the frosty air. After a moment, when Sasha still did not respond. He spoke again.

'I wanted to tell you something,' he said.

'What?'

'After tonight, I'm done. I promise.'

He waited on edge to hear her response.

'I've forgiven you,' she said.

Rehan closed his eyes and nodded in approval. There was still some acidity in her tone.

'How did you know it was me?' he asked.

'Pretty apparent, wasn't it? I was at his apartment the next day,' she said. 'My picture on the fridge was gone. I found a card of your Company in my dad's coat pocket. I must say it was very careless of you. I was going through a bad time myself, so I too made the call. And then when you came to me suddenly after all these years and told me about yourself…I figured it out.'

'I am sorry,' said Rehan as he looked out at the sprawling city landscape which shaped an outline amidst the grey industrialized buildings. 'But you never told me why…'

A click on the other end left him all alone in the dark. He still had no idea why Sasha wanted to die. But for now, she was alive and that is all that mattered.

❚❚❚

Rehan had finally managed to take a quick nap before his hit tonight. Now as he waited for Arif's call, he watched TV with a blank expression. He surveyed the table where his gun sat. The

TV continued as a cluttered background noise, while Rehan reached over and slowly picked up the gun. He examined it and ran his hand slowly and intricately over the barrel feeling the grain of the metal.

A thunderous knock on the door startled him. He placed the gun down, turned off the TV and stood to get the door. Before he could reach it, the knob was turned and Arif let himself in.

'Shit Arif, you could wait till I got the door,' Rehan said.

'Fuck no. You know what the temperature outside is?'

Arif made his way to the kitchen, where he pulled out two beers from the refrigerator. He came over to the couch and handed one to Rehan. Both of them opened it and took a giant gulp.

'I'm done,' said Rehan abruptly.

'With Sasha?' Arif inquired.

'No, with my job.'

Arif gawked at him like he was crazy. He sipped his beer and laid it down before clearing his throat.

'Excuse me?' he said.

'Tonight's my last night,' Rehan said staring out into nothingness.

Arif scratched his brow and took a moment to excogitate. Finally he spoke.

'These people want to die, we're helping them.'

'Are we really?' asked Rehan.

'Come on, we'll talk to the Colonel, he'll know what to say. It's a phase, snap out of it.'

'It's not a phase,' said Rehan. 'I'm done after tonight.'

'Then what are you going to do?'

Rehan leaned back on his couch, blinking a few times. He took his time answering Arif.

'I got a cousin up in Delhi who said he could hook me up with a job. The starting pay is substantially less, but I won't feel like a dirtbag every night,' said Rehan

Arif moved in closer and looked at him.

'Hey, look at me,' he said. 'You're not a dirtbag. These people had the same opportunities and they are making the same conscious decision. The choice that you chose not to take when you joined us.'

Arif finished of his beer in a victorious fashion as Rehan glared at him.

'I'm done,' he reiterated.

'So you're done. Now what? So after tonight, you will just pick up and leave?'

'I'm going on a spiritual self-journey,' Rehan said.

Arif gaped at him in disbelief. His eyes narrowed suspiciously.

'What the hell is that?' he asked. 'Like jacking off? Because that is spiritual and self-satisfying.'

'God damn it Arif, I want to try and find myself, or God, or something. Somehow. You know?' Rehan said.

'You want to find God... Honestly?' Arif asked sarcastically.

Rehan remained silent as he took in the change in tone.

'Yeah, I do,' he said.

'Well, then take some acid man...'

Arif's phone went off. He pulled it out to check it. There were two text messages from Colonel Puri in his inbox.

'The assignment details are here,' he told Rehan and read the first message.

Client's Name – Sagar Shinde

Location – Penthouse, B-Wing, Smruti Heritage, Near Lady of Salvation Church, Gokhale Road, Dadar West.

The message was pretty straight forward. He went over to the next message and opened it. It read…

Arif, my son, here comes the important part. You might have reservations about eliminating your next target but it is of utmost importance to our company. The name of the next target is – Rehan Irani.

He looked around and gulped. Then continued…

He has gone soft and has fallen in love with a client which is against company policy. At some point he will ask us to leave and that will put our secrecy in jeopardy. I expect you to eliminate him at the hit location. We will take care of the girl later. Don't let emotions distract you or else you won't be able to pull the trigger. Best of luck.

Arif couldn't believe what he had read. His boss had just asked him to kill his best friend and he was right in his understanding of the situation. Rehan had just told him about his decision to quit. But there was no way he could do it. But then could he double-cross his boss, his wife's brother? He looked at Rehan who sat next to him looking up at the ceiling, completely unaware of the turmoil that might leave either of them in ruins.

Emotions were getting the better of Arif and it was almost impossible for him to utter anything. This was his choice now, and man how he hated choices. Thankfully for him, Rehan came out of his trance.

'Time to go?' he asked him.

'Yes,' said Arif.

14th June 2013

Set in the heart of Dadar and spread over an acre of land, the Smruti Heritage was a housing society comprising seven wings. Their scouting trips had shown that each wing had fourteen floors and the three entrances to the society were guarded by security personnel. It was a posh setting and commanded a certain attention from the surroundings. A police patrol car would drive past the road in front every fifteen minutes or so. The Colonel had been right with his warning; this was not going to be a cakewalk.

Arif and Rehan waited on the dark curbside in the car near the B wing entrance mulling about their next move. While Rehan observed the surrounding and planned for a way to break in, Arif was fighting his own inner demons. As he looked at Rehan, he had no idea what he was going to do. For the longest time possible now, Rehan was the only one he had close to a friend. How could he do this to him? Would he be able to live with himself after that? But every time he thought about telling Rehan the truth, the thought of upsetting the Colonel popped right back up. And each time that fear triumphed over his loyalty.

'Something doesn't feel right,' Rehan said still looking at the society vacantly.

'I know,' said Arif.

Rehan wondered if it was best to scale the wall or take the car inside. Scaling the wall would provide with an unobtrusive entry but the escape would become difficult if something went awry. On the other hand, entering with a car would be difficult, as they had no alibi. Escape would be easy if they entered unnoticed because then the guards would confuse the vehicle to be from the colony. Yes, that was what he had to do. Patience.

In a few minutes Rehan saw the guard at an entrance desert his post, as if called by someone.

'Quick, drive to that last entrance,' he signalled to Arif. 'Don't be rash.'

Arif followed his orders and drove the car steadily to the last entrance. Confirming that the post was empty, they drove in. They motored up to the B wing and headed down into the underground parking. There weren't many cars parked in the huge parking lot and that allowed Arif to park the car in a spot very close to the elevator.

'Let's make this quick,' said Rehan as they approached the elevator and headed upstairs.

Arif still was at a loss for words. He could not figure out any way to get past this peculiar situation he found himself in. And he knew that nothing he said was going to make a difference. The elevator arrived on the fourteenth floor and the men moved out of it. A small corridor led to one single door of the penthouse on the floor. Fluorescent tube lights illuminated the passage in alternate bands of light and dark.

Arif grabbed the doorknob, turned it and pushed the door open. The room inside was pitch dark. They couldn't spot anything.

'Too dark, pull out your flashlight. I'll follow you,' Rehan said tersely.

Arif pulled out his gun and stepped into the house as he fumbled in his pocket for the flashlight. He was directly underneath the doorframe as Rehan slowly followed behind. Arif took a step past the edge of the door to where the light from the corridor spilled in the room and before he could pull his hand out of his pocket, a flash and ear splitting noise of a gunshot galvanized Rehan. He immediately took cover behind the door as Arif, with his hand still in his pocket, stood still, barely visible in the dim light.

'Fuck Arif, the Colonel asked us to use the silencer,' he said.

Arif turned, his eyes wide, showed his gun in the fluorescent wash; it still had the long thin silencer attached. Then he swayed and slumped to the ground lifeless as blood spurted through his chest. A bullet had flown straight through his heart. Rehan crouched stupefied for a second; aghast at what he was seeing. Heart already in his mouth, the first signs of panic drifting in… Then muffled footsteps were heard in the dark as a silhouette approached him and he instinctively slammed the door into the shape. A crunch was heard as it made contact with the man. Rehan bent down, grabbed the man's leg and gave it a swift pull. The man crashed into the floor and the gun spiralled out of his hand, landing in the lighted triangle but before Rehan could capitalize, one of his flailing legs caught him square in the jaw. The man then scrambled straight and kicked him in the chest.

He then reached for the gun, when Rehan recognized the man from a picture he had seen as he tried to pull his gun out of his coat pocket. Mr. Shinde bent down for the gun but before he could reach it, Rehan put a bullet through his knee, pulled him closer and slammed his knee into Shinde's chest as he climbed to straddle him. Rehan then put his gun right on the man's forehead.

'Fuck you...What the fuck are you doing?' asked Rehan flustered and shocked.

Mister Shinde trembled as blood dripped from his mouth as the gun indented his forehead. He mouthed something but no words came out.

'Are you fucking saying something?' asked Rehan.

'I changed my mind,' croaked the man. 'I don't want to die.' His voice was barely audible.

Rehan took a deep breath and looked at the door. The lights in the hallway lightened up Arif's lifeless face. At that moment, mercy definitely wasn't on his side and considering the rising voices from the floor below, neither was time.

'Too late brother, too late,' Rehan said as he pulled the man's coat over his head to avoid any blood spill on him and fired a bullet in the dead centre.

He stood completely still for a moment and looked out over the scene. Arif's body lay on the ground sprawled out as his eyes stared blankly at the pale white ceiling. He didn't have time but he had to take Arif's body with him. Arif would have done the same. Rehan ran over to him and grabbed his body checking for his vitals; there were none. He was dead for sure. He ran to the window, pulled down the curtain and spreading it on the ground, rolled Arif's body onto it. He took his gun and put it in his pocket and started dragging him out of the house and towards the elevator. Thankfully, the thick curtain prevented a bloody trail. He pushed the button calling for it and ran back to the penthouse, switched on the TV at a high volume, closed the door and ran back finishing all of this in two minutes. He then pulled the body into the elevator and pressed the 'Close Door' button and the 'Basement' button together for five seconds to descend towards the basement without stopping along the way and having anybody else see the body with him. This was a feature built in most elevators to enable firemen to reach their desired floors without stopping.

A gunshot had been fired in the middle of the night. Rehan knew that people would have heard it, but most of them wouldn't react much considering the TV was now on. But he couldn't take chances. As he reached the basement, he could hear the guards whistle for the police at a level above him. As he exited the elevator, he could hear the voices of people, some in panic. That meant trouble and he knew it, but he could not leave Arif's body behind. He dragged the corpse to the car and plunged it into the car's trunk. Rehan rushed to a tap nearby, splashed some water on his face and got rid of the blood on his hands. Finally he pulled himself into the driver's seat and quietly drove out of the underground parking and took a right turn towards the third exit near E block.

As he drove by, he saw a telltale red strobe light at the B block gate of the society. Rehan knew that his escape would be difficult, but he couldn't rush. There was no chance in hell that he was just going to drive out without being noticed. The felly turn of events hindered his capacity to think straight but he couldn't panic. All this had never been in the script. But he had to think. He took a few deep breaths when a plan started formulating in his mind. Mobs were always stupid and he could slip right past the most guarded exit. A plan so overt that it was covert. He turned back towards the B wing exit, near to where the people stood, turned off the car's engine and looked out the window. The gunshot had obviously attracted them to the scene. Rehan looked at his reflection in the rear view mirror. Dressed up in a black suit and white shirt, he certainly did not look like an assassin. He examined his hands and clothes to see if there were any traces of blood; there were none. After taking a deep breath and steadying himself, he got out of the car and walked casually towards the crowd.

'What happened brother? What is all the fuss about?' he calmly asked one of the men standing there.

'There has been a shootout in this building,' the man said.

'No way,' Rehan exclaimed, intentionally overacting. 'Who got shot?'

'We don't know yet,' said the man. 'The police have just arrived.'

A police constable walked up to the crowd while other officials rushed into the building.

'We suspect the shooter to still be in the building,' he said. 'All of you are requested to go back to your houses. It is not safe out here.'

Rehan walked over to the constable with a solemn expression on his face and talked to him earnestly.

'Sir, my name is Tushar Rao,' Rehan lied. 'I live in the D wing. Sir, I have a flight to catch in two hours for London. I was just driving out in my car out there. Am I allowed to go sir? I have a very important meeting to attend,' Rehan concluded lamentably.

The constable's chest broadened with pride. Such well dressed guys seldom spoke with respect and that made him mellow down a bit.

'Yes, yes, you can go. Do good work there and help this country from whatever crap is happening here,' he told Rehan. 'Let this man go,' he shouted out to the guards at the gate.

'Thank you, sir. Thank you very much,' Rehan said and shook the constable's hand.

He walked back to the car, got in and coolly drove out of Smruti Heritage without any flurry. Even though the emotions were getting the better of him as he thought about his friend lying dead in the trunk of the car, Rehan could not help but be amused by the comedy of the situation.

What an idiot! he thought. A smile crept up at the corner of his lips and tears rolled down from his eyes as he escaped into the night.

❚ ❚ ❚

The sound of thunder echoed through the city and flashes of lightening lit up the sky. A slight drizzle had just begun as Rehan pulled up his car outside Colonel Puri's bungalow, not remembering how he got there. There was another storm brewing up within him, his multitude of feelings wrestling each other. He fought hard to restrain his tears as he picked up his phone and called the Colonel.

Colonel Puri was wide-awake and was sitting in his study. He answered the phone on the third ring.

'Hello…Rehan?' he said.

'Would you please come down Colonel?' Rehan said. 'I am waiting outside your house.'

The Colonel got a bit anxious. Obviously Rehan wasn't dead like he wanted him to be. He wondered if he had found out about his intentions to kill him.

'I will be right down,' Colonel Puri said and hung up. He then walked up to the fireplace and swung the painting above it to reveal a hidden safe. He pulled out a silenced Walther and hid it in his waistband.

Rehan waited in the car. The events of tonight were recreating themselves inside his head. He thought hard about them; maybe there was something he could have done to save Arif. He searched for that something but nothing came.

A couple of minutes later, the main gate of the bungalow opened and Colonel Puri emerged from it. He stood on the pavement wearing a black nightgown, white pyjamas and carrying an umbrella. Rehan got out of the car and not caring for the rain, walked up to him.

'What happened?' the Colonel asked; his tone all confused and worried.

'Arif...got shot. Arif got fucking shot,' Rehan said. His voice was cracking up.

'What? How?' The Colonel almost yelled as he grabbed onto Rehan's collar but then sobered up saying, 'Okay, let's get in the car and talk.'

'The target went rogue. He opened fire at us. And then there were cops...' Rehan rambled on mechanically opening the door and sitting down.

As Rehan narrated the details to the Colonel, everything around him seemed to dissolve. The voices faded away and the entire conversation drowned out. He could see the Colonel's lips moving but he could not comprehend his questions. Then the colonel placed his hand on Rehan's shoulder, which woke him up a bit and asked about the body.

A detached expression overtook his face as he said, 'It's in the trunk.'

'Okay, I'll open the gate, you drive in and enter the garage. The door is open. Wait for me in the car.'

Rehan drove inside as the Colonel made sure no one was around and looking and then closed the main gate behind him.

⬤ ⬤ ⬤

The rising sun hadn't yet appeared at the horizon. The vicinity was quiet and the rain continued to pour down. Arif's classy house sat on a slight hill in the nice neighbourhood of Breach Candy. The rain had created puddles of water in the front lawn. Colonel Puri squelched across the wet grass leading to the door.

He walked as slowly as possible and stopped momentarily at the door. After knocking it three times, he took a step back fearing the ordeal that awaited him. He would be direct, as usual.

The door swung open. Priya stood there with a shawl wrapped around herself and a confused look on her face. The Colonel nodded at her and she sincerely nodded back.

'Hi brother, what brings you over?' she asked. 'Come in, for goodness' sake, you'll catch a cold.'

Colonel Puri shook his head and stood his ground in the pouring rain.

'I come with bad news,' he said.

Priya looked at him even more confused and leaned up against the wall. The Colonel opened his mouth; about to speak but abruptly closed it.

'There's no easy way to say...' he began.

'Spit it out, what's wrong?' Priya asked.

'It's... it's Arif; he was...killed last night,' Colonel Puri broke the news.

Silence filled the void. He could see Priya breathing heavily as she allowed the news to sink in.

'He and Rehan were out walking back and they decided to take a shortcut. A few goons tried to rob them.' The Colonel paused briefly as he ran over the formulated story in his mind again. 'When Arif refused, they shot him. Rehan barely managed to get out alive.'

Priya emitted a loud wail and clapped her hands over her mouth. The blow had hit its mark and all that could be seen was the shattering effect. Tears flowed from her eyes and she lost all control over herself as she crashed into the Colonel's arms in palpable shock. All he could do was stand there like a mannequin. He had no condolences to lend.

▌▌▌

A shade of grey engulfed Rehan's bedroom. The sun hid itself behind a dark cloud cover and the rain showed no signs of stopping. Rehan lay on his bed, afraid to close his eyes. He stared out at nothing, lost in thought and yet trying to stop himself from thinking. The struggle with himself was wearing him out.

His alarm clock buzzed to his immediate response. It was ten minutes past eight in the morning when he slammed it off, before returning to his vacant position. He hadn't slept all night. How could he have? With every passing second, the pain became more intense. Everything was so fresh in his mind. Wishing he could selectively remove memories, he turned on his side, realizing that he would have to erase most of his life to attain peace. The fragility of life had always intrigued him, his business being a merciless killer. He always thought about all the hopes, aspirations and the commitments that a person stood for, vanishing in moments. *So easy to take a life and yet so difficult to build one.* But never once, since the death of his mother had he felt this sense of loss so close to himself and it somehow mingled with the pain he had felt then, increasing it exponentially. His father had been aloof long enough for him to not feel the snap. But this...this was different even from a child's trauma. This included a strain of helplessness and the lost chance of perhaps saving Arif that made him think of killing himself too. But he wasn't going to cut himself with that knife called guilt. Easier said than done. 'Survivor's guilt,' they termed it. Fucking true.

Rehan finally decided to get off his arse and take a stroll. He walked over into the living room and played some music on his stereo loud enough to drown his thoughts, but failed miserably. No matter how hard he tried to feel a little upbeat, his legs just refused to move. So he walked to the couch and plopped down. He sat there motionlessly listening to the Bollywood music that played on the speakers before picking up his phone. There were a few missed calls on it from Sasha since last night. Neither did he have the will to call her back nor the desire to talk to anyone. Instead he closed his eyes, leaned back against the couch and drifted off into his own thoughts.

▌▌▌

Colonel Puri sat at the dining table with his wife finishing his breakfast. The woman had a look of despair as she stared at him, sadly.

'Going to work early today,' he told her.

'So what happened with Arif?' she asked him.

The Colonel sighed and glanced up at her, never making eye-contact. He shook his head glumly.

'I told you last night. He was mugged,' he said.

'I know that, but have the police found any leads?'

'They're not going to find any leads,' the Colonel said assertively.

Mrs. Puri's attention moved to the window and she was distressed. She turned back directly at him.

'Sad, sad thing to lose a life. How is Priya taking it?' she asked.

'Pretty okay. She'll be fine in due time. I have already told her of my plans to look after her child's future. She wasn't really listening then, but I guess she'll come around.'

His wife smiled a painful smile at her caring husband but he couldn't handle that expression anymore. He had deceived enough people in his life and it had started getting to him. Secrets apparently had their cost.

The grey skies on the outside looked daunting and yet darkly beautiful.

'I gotta go,' he said and headed out.

❚ ❚ ❚

Rehan was lying down on his couch and staring at his lap, a pained expression etched on his face, tasting salt in his mouth. He had no idea what time it was and how long he had been like this but a niggling pain in his back suggested that it had been quite long.

Rehan's phone rang again like it had a couple of times already this morning. After having ignored it all this while, this time around he slowly reached out and with no energy, picked it up on the fifth ring.

'Yeah?'

'Rehan?' It was Sasha.

'Yeah.'

'I really want to see you. I need to see you. I just talked to Priya…' she said. 'What happened with Arif?'

Rehan's voice was hardly audible. 'He was mugged,' he looked helplessly at his reflection in the television screen as he whispered this lie.

❚ ❚ ❚

Rehan and Sasha turned around the corner and walked towards the Gateway of India in the rain, under one umbrella. He peered over at her and she stared ahead, not acknowledging his look.

'I still think there's more to the story,' she said.

He began telling her the story again 'We were walking back…'

'I don't want to hear it again,' she interrupted. 'And that's why I know you're lying. It's too clichéd and you remember the story too well.'

Rehan stopped in his tracks as she continued walking. He looked at her, baffled by her remark. She spoke from ahead.

'So, are you going to tell me the real story?'

He stood rooted to his spot. Little drops of water trickled down on his face. She kept walking, without turning around. After a second, he picked up his pace and caught up with her.

'It is the real story,' he said.

'Priya told me. She believes it,' said Sasha and then looked at him. 'But I know you're lying.'

Rehan allowed that awkward moment to pass. He pulled out a cigarette and tried to light it a few times.

'His funeral is tomorrow. I'm making a speech,' he said and paused briefly as he took a drag from his cigarette. 'And the worst part of it all is... I don't feel like I'm the right person to give a speech for him.'

'Why not?'

'I'm...I'm not prepared. I feel almost guilty giving the speech,' he said.

'So there is more,' Sasha opined

Rehan, entranced by the ground, barely nodded. He then gazed right into her eyes.

'I didn't tell the truth. Not to Priya, not to you and not even to myself,' he said being cryptic. It was his only choice. He knew this would all crash on him later but he couldn't deal with it all right now.

His eyes became slightly glazed before he broke eye contact with her and looked down at the ground.

❚❚❚

Rehan and Sasha lay on the bed in his apartment. Lying under the cover, Rehan had his arm around her and spoke quietly into her ear.

'I really like holding you. The way your heart beats against mine; your breath, warm and cool at the same time,' he said. 'It makes me feel...feel...I don't know. It just makes me feel.'

She let out a quiet laugh, turned around and kissed Rehan on his forehead. He showed a small pained smile.

'You won't tell Priya the truth, will you?' he asked. 'It'll kill her and destroy so many bonds. I promise you she won't want to know the truth...'

Sasha cut him off midway.

'Everyone wants to hear the truth,' she said as she ran her hand over his shirt. 'She might regret the truth, but she would want to know.'

'She doesn't know what we do,' said Rehan. 'There's almost no one who knows what we do.'

'I promised you I would not tell anyone. I will keep my word.'

Rehan was silent. He allowed himself to feel this moment. He allowed himself to feel the love of his life close to him. He also wanted to allow himself to feel some of the joy he had rarely felt and was still failing to. Finally, after a few seconds, he spoke.

'I don't know what all this means anymore. I don't know what to do with my being, with my time.'

'Didn't you have it all figured out?' she asked.

'No, never in fact was I sure of my life. Always been like driftwood but at least now I know I'll never have it all figured out. Not completely. This one percent of doubt will eat me alive,' he said and looked down at her. She lay next to him with her head resting on his chest. 'The only thing that I have absolutely figured out is that I love you.'

Sasha looked up at him. A smile appeared on her face.

'This has been a long time coming, hasn't it?' she asked.

'Nope,' he said. 'It has always been there. For almost ten years. It has always been there.'

Sasha pulled herself up and sat next to him. She leant in closer and looked deeply into his eyes.

'Say it again.' she said.

Rehan smirked and said it. 'Sasha Fernandez, I love you.'

'I love you too,' said Sasha and wrapped her arm around him. He allowed her to draw closer and place her lips on his. The softness of her lips, the warm breath with the cool wetness almost ecstatic, until passion consumed everything but the presence of the other in increasing states of entanglement without realization. Almost an absence of the self; if something was close to meditation, this probably was.

It was everything he had ever imagined and so much more. All day long he had been hurting. All day long he had been waiting for some relief from it. It was at that very moment when he felt it. This was his moment of joy, of peace.

A small group of people had assembled outside the electric crematorium in Shivaji Park. The funeral service was about to begin. The overnight showers had created shallow puddles of water on the ground reflecting the bleak grey sky. A long cardboard box was placed on a pedestal next to the crematory. A small crowd was gathered none of whom Rehan could place, so he kept his distance.

Slowly he made his way to the front with Sasha as they saw a brown flimsy looking box about six feet long lying on a pedestal covered by a shed.

'What is that?' he asked.

'It looks like cardboard,' she said.

They looked at each other perplexed as Colonel Puri walked in behind them holding Priya's arm. Tears dribbled down Priya's face as she nodded at them. Sasha gave her a hug.

'I'm so, so sorry for the loss,' she told her.

Rehan awkwardly hung back. He couldn't bear the small talk and so veered over towards the Colonel while Priya and Sasha talked.

'Arif... in the cardboard box?' he asked him.

'Yes.'

Rehan nodded at his answer a few times, waiting for more of an explanation.

'Yeah, he wanted to die in an eco-friendly way,' the Colonel said. 'That's what he told Priya once. It cheered her up a little bit. Good to see a smile.'

'Yes, definitely,' said Rehan as all of them gathered around for Arif's last rites.

Priya couldn't have managed to say anything through her tears as she clung on to Arif's mother who had come to see her son. His dad had passed away already. All alone, Rehan tried to imagine how the lady was feeling. The worst possible thing to happen to someone in his regard and so the Colonel took over with his small eulogy. Succinct and calm, he delivered how great a person lay before them and how even the most frivolous of things can shatter a life, giving a message to enjoy what we have, when we have it, just like Arif, always jovial, always good humoured. He then stepped down from the pedestal and it was Rehan's turn. He wished his voice to be as calm as the Colonel's. It almost had a soothing effect but he knew he wouldn't be able to manage. He finally pulled himself together, at least enough to climb the pedestal.

He cleared his throat looking at the sobbing people, his eyes already watering at the sight, he croaked.

'Here lies the stopped heart of a man who made a point to always live by it. It was the overtime I think that made his heart resign. My constant, in fact, my only companion for the past few years who had always pulled me through thick and thin. One rarely finds such people in their life who would stand, not beside, but in front of you in an attempt to shield you from whatever may come. A clean and peaceful soul, who even through his innumerable swear words always portrayed an aura of good natured humour, whom I will sorely miss all my life. So on this day when God possibly needed his entertainment and spirit more than we did, I'd say one word in the lines of Arif. Well... Fuck!'

Rehan broke down on the box, almost bending it in the process as the Colonel hurried up to extricate him from the place, all the while condoling him. Through hazy eyes, Rehan saw Arif's mother muster the guts to say something but he couldn't focus until at last the conveyer whirred and took the box to its fiery end.

To Rehan it almost felt like being dragged to hell. He definitely didn't want to go that way, eco friendly or not.

▌▌▌

The funeral had been pretty okay; at least that is what Rehan thought. Everything had proceeded smoothly and he had even managed to deliver his speech. Sure he was still hurting a little bit, but he knew that it wasn't something he couldn't handle. And to make things easier on himself, he had decided to spend the afternoon with Sasha at her apartment. Lying on the tattered sofa in the living room, he stared stupefied at the blank wall in front of him. Sasha was slumped against a chair and looked around the room silently. He needed to get off the life he led... but how? He couldn't just run away. But then, why not?

'You know what?' Rehan asked her.

'What?'

'We should leave. Just go,' he said.

'What?'

'We should just leave town and go somewhere else,' he clarified.

'Where?' she asked.

'I don't know, maybe Delhi? Maybe not.'

'You want a change?' Sasha asked him as she finally sat back up straight.

'I need a change,' said Rehan.

Sasha waited for a second. She realized that perhaps he was being serious here. After giving it some thought, she took a deep breath and looked directly at him.

'Weren't you the one who told me not to run from my problems?'

'I'm not running from my problems,' said Rehan. 'Wanting to die, or killing yourself is running from problems. I'm trying something new. Change. Keeping the idea alive that there is still something.'

Sasha got up from her chair and stood still. Rehan braced himself for more negative words. Strangely, she looked at him with a smile, walked towards him and kneeled down on the floor next to him.

'When do we go?' she asked stroking his hair amicably.

Rehan nodded and bit his lower lip.

'I love you,' he said peering into her eyes.

'I love you too.'

❚ ❚ ❚

A few metres down the liveliness of the market ran a small dingy alley welcoming its visitors with the acrobatics of rats zipping in and out of crevices. This was where life tired of its retinue tried to find a feeble escape but folded into itself. There was a door at the other end of the alley with a dim light coming from inside. A patchy sign, obviously not looked after, hung at an angle from the door, creaking in the wind, as ominous a sound as the people inside, read - The Garage Pub.

Out from around the corner, a woman bundled up in a red hoodie and black pants trekked towards the pub. She slowly reached the door and entered. Covering her hand with a pulled up sleeve, she pushed the door open.

It was a shady place filled with the refuse of the city, brown smoke emanating from some corner among stupefied eyes while the chink of glasses led to another corner of sloshed stinkers. She slowly circled the edge before seeing a tall, bald black man, standing by a group watching as they heated powders in spoons. The man turned around and caught her eye. He signalled for her to come closer. She moved towards him capturing the eyes of most men at the bar.

'Sit,' he said as he pulled a chair.

She took a seat next to him and removed her hood to reveal her curly hair. The obvious attention she was receiving bothered Sasha. The man sitting next to her shifted and stared at her for a second, taking in her restlessness.

'I knew you'd see me again Sasha,' said the man.

'This is my last time,' she said. 'I'm moving… starting over.'

The man let out a mix between a laugh and a grunt. He shook his head in disbelief at her.

'Haven't I heard that before? But they all return…' he said and continued. 'You think if you move, it will stop everything? Life will just change magically?'

Sasha sat in silence; absorbing his words, her attention focused at the ground.

'You're a dumb bitch,' the man continued. 'Moving changes nothing. I've moved over seven times and I'm the same fuck up as I always was. You don't run. You can't run.'

Sasha still had no words and she merely continued to concentrate on the ground. He noticed that and spoke once more.

'So you think you will run away... and then what? The new Sasha will emerge from her coke lined cocoon and spread her wings? She won't need the stuff she has been relying on? Man, even biting nails takes longer to get rid of.'

She still didn't stir, her eyes rooted to the same spot. The man looked at her, disgusted.

'So that's it? Silence... you got nothing to say?' he asked.

'I am moving,' she said. 'It may not change anything but I am leaving. I have to.'

'So you are a new person, huh, why are you here then?'

Sasha still stared down at the ground, not making eye contact with the man. She muttered something inaudible.

'What? I couldn't hear you?' the man said.

She looked up at him, ashamed and broken down before she mumbled quietly.

'You know why.'

'Okay,' he softened. 'Come with me.'

He quickly stood up but she remained seated, deflated. The man began to walk away. He turned around to look at her. She finally stood with no energy and dragged her feet to follow him.

❚❚❚

It hadn't rained all day but the threat still lingered making the whole effect quite pleasant. Under the street lights the city of Mumbai glowed with animation and sprightliness in the air. Colonel Puri's gigantic bungalow loomed higher than the surrounding buildings as making a mark on the landscape. The front door opened as he came out of his house wearing a heavy coat and walked over to his car as it beeped in response to its master's presence. He pulled his car out of the driveway as the guard hurried to open the main gate and left his house in the background.

The Colonel drove his Jaguar while listening to some swing manouche looking to be in a lively mood. He stopped at a red light all the while his fingers twirling to the music on the steering wheel and then continued down the road. The traffic wasn't heavy and it took him about twenty minutes to reach the High Street Phoenix Mall. Colonel Puri waited outside the entrance of the mall for about three minutes when the passenger door opened and Rehan entered the car. They silently nodded at each other as the music mellowed down to a cello bass.

After parking the car in the basement parking lot, they headed towards Tryst hoping the place could live up to its name and smoothen the jagged edges between them. Tryst was a night club situated inside the far reaches of the mall. Two bulky looking bouncers dressed in black and a manager guarded the gate. Colonel Puri walked up to them and confirmed his reservation.

'Yes sir, your table is ready,' said the manager after checking their names on the list. One of the bouncers escorted them inside.

The clangour of house music filled the room and a sea of people grooved to the music on a glossy dance floor. The evening at Tryst felt like a spectacular light show; about a million colour changing LEDs poked out of almost every corner and the bright green absinthe potions swirling around in glasses gave it an almost spaceship like appearance. The focus of this futuristically designed club was the elevated VIP tables and they made their way towards one such table, sidling through the crowd.

Rehan sat himself in the VIP booth overlooking the dance floor as people writhed about constantly, but he merely sat gazing out of the window. The Colonel walked over and placed a beer down in front of him as he took the seat right opposite.

'Thanks,' said Rehan.

The Colonel nodded and looked out across the dance floor. He smiled and shifted back towards Rehan, who stared down into his beer.

'Why are we here?' he asked.

'We are here for Arif,' said the Colonel. 'All his life the man was jovial and loved to put a smile on everyone's face. I thought remembering him this way instead of mourning might make him feel better up there.'

'Hmm,' muttered Rehan and raised his beer to toast. 'To Arif then.'

'To Arif,' said the Colonel and both men took a sip of their beers. 'This is what life is all about,' Colonel Puri continued. 'Sipping good alcohol and getting the best table in the most crowded club in the city. Being rich surely has its benefits.'

A rare smile had appeared on his face, which Rehan had never seen before. He seemed to have a part of Arif within himself.

'Am I supposed to congratulate you here?' Rehan quipped.

The Colonel let out a forced laugh and sank back into his chair.

'So, any plans with Sasha?' he asked.

'Um, not tonight. But tomorrow we have big plans.'

The Colonel looked at him suspiciously, took a large swig of the beer and slammed it down.

'You know, I'm still going to ask her if she wants to live,' he said.

'She does,' Rehan said assertively.

'Well, I'll just have to ask her, won't I?'

Rehan simply turned away and sipped his beer. He avoided eye contact with Puri.

'Listen Rehan,' the Colonel spoke as he leaned in towards him. 'I know you've got some stuff to get off. I know you're damn well planning to do something drastic, I know it. I don't know what it is, but let me be clear to you. If our company is found out about, we will both be behind bars, so...'

Rehan cut him off midway. 'No, no. I'm not planning anything like that. I swear.'

That somehow made the Colonel's face soften and even a small smile formed.

'I know you're a man of your word, Rehan,' he said. 'If nothing else, I know that about you.'

Colonel Puri held up a finger, indicating one second. He got up and left the booth. Rehan saw him head over to another table on the opposite side of the club and greet a few elderly guys dressed up elegantly. The Colonel chatted up with them for a couple of minutes before returning with four beers. He slid two beers at Rehan and sat down. Rehan didn't bother asking him who the people were and just opened his beer and took a gulp from it.

'So you were saying that you have plans,' said the Colonel. 'What are you planning to do?'

'Nothing...just leave,' said Rehan.

Colonel Puri paused as he processed these words. He firmly stared at him.

'Can't say I didn't suspect it,' he said. 'Do you have any plans kid, anywhere to go?'

Rehan tore his gaze from the Colonel out onto the lively dance floor.

'I don't know,' he said. 'I guess I have no plans, I really don't know. I'll just be. You know? It'll just be… me and Sasha.'

Colonel Puri shook his head in disapproval. He finished his beer clean in two large gulps. Rehan saw this and then looked down at his half full beer.

'It doesn't work like that. It never has, never will,' said the Colonel. 'You need a goddamn plan in life. How the fuck do you think you're going to succeed?'

Rehan merely avoided Puri's heated gaze. He chewed on his tongue when a very gorgeous woman walked up to them carrying a bottle of Glenfiddich single malt whiskey, two ornate glasses and the works.

'Enjoy, sir,' she said after placing it down on the table.

'Thanks,' said the Colonel.

The waitress turned and walked away. Colonel Puri stared at her disappearing figure for a while before he spoke.

'So, let us drink some more,' he said, then added winking, 'But first I'd like it if you keep up young man.'

He poured two large pegs in two glasses and passed one to Rehan who reluctantly took it astride as he chugged his beer.

'Bottoms up,' said the Colonel and gulped down his drink quickly.

Rehan, astounded for a second, quickly followed suit. A dizzy feeling overtook him and he shook his head vigorously in an attempt to get rid of it. The feeling did not go away and only became worse. The alcohol was definitely taking its toll. Mr. Puri seemed to have some agenda today and Rehan allowed the flavour to set in before he spoke again.

'You know, I think it could work,' he said.

'What could?' the Colonel asked.

'Moving away with Sasha…starting from scratch.'

Colonel Puri nodded. He too was getting a little tipsy.

'Yeah, no, you're right, it's a wonderful idea,' he said condescendingly. 'Take two people, both with undeniable loneliness and depression problems and let them loose in an unforgiving world. It sounds like a brilliant plan,' the sarcasm patently evident from his tone. 'So no plans, no fucking clue as to where you're leaving for?'

He poured himself another peg and glared at Rehan. Colonel Puri shot this one straight down his throat as well. The alcohol burned his insides and made him grimace. But being the sot that he was, he had no intentions of stopping today. He now spoke with more menace.

'Three days ago this chick was on the verge of fucking killing herself,' he said. 'You know this. I don't need to remind you, right?'

'No,' said Rehan.

'And now your idea is to hold on to a suicidal case for who cares what reasons and take her away from everything she knows into the unknown and just hope you two float?'

The Colonel leaned towards Rehan; his temper was rising a little. The drunken belligerence was surely beginning to kick in.

'You realize what I'm saying,' he continued. 'Let her go, damn it. Move on, you're already fucked. You don't need someone even worse off than you in your life right now.'

Rehan mumbled something inaudible under his breath. The Colonel gave him a confused stare.

'What? Speak up son, couldn't hear you,' he said.

Rehan looked directly into Colonel Puri's eyes and spoke up boldly.

'I said, maybe the unknown is the cure for her. Since everything she knows turned her suicidal.'

The Colonel was taken aback. He blinked a few times and hung his head.

'And plus it's not just for her,' Rehan continued. 'It's for me too. I need the unknown, I need something new. It has all become stagnant now. I can't handle it anymore. I'll rot…'

Colonel Puri was definitely perplexed with Rehan's forthrightness. He leaned back and slumped into the sofa. After a few seconds he reached over, grabbed the whiskey bottle and took a straight pull.

'I need something new, I just feel trapped. You know?' Rehan said. His voice was full of desperation and his eyes were looking for the Colonel's approval. He knew the Colonel would hunt him down if he didn't agree to his proposition.

Colonel Puri veered his gaze from the ground to Rehan.

'We all feel trapped, kid,' he said. 'Moving won't change that, dying will.'

He took a large pull directly from the bottle and passed it to Rehan who looked at the bottle for a second before taking it and gulping the contents down.

❚❚❚

Rehan stumbled into his apartment and collapsed on the couch. He didn't remember how he had reached there and neither did he care. His head was spinning and the world seemed to spin along, from the right to the left and returning inexplicably to its starting point without completing a whole revolution. He was clearly drunk. He stared at the TV, which was turned off. He looked up at the ceiling, down at the ground and all around. It felt like he did not recognize anything in the room. Finally he kicked his centre table hard, making it fly into the wall. He grabbed a cup and threw it into the window, smashing the glass pares on the balcony. He then punched the wall angrily and fell back on the couch and looked around the room taking in the change. The footsteps of humanity were always destructive.

Still obviously outraged, he saw his pistol on the kitchen counter and stumbled towards it. These furious actions were only disguised outlets, rarely helping to vent the emotions as they welled up inside him. He reached out and cautiously picked it up.

'Hello. Look at this fucker,' Rehan said and looked directly down the barrel. He rubbed the gun along his forehead.

Moving won't change anything, dying will. The Colonel's words were echoing inside his head and Rehan couldn't fight that niggling urge any more.

'Time for a change then,' he said.

Rehan raised the pistol and placed the barrel inside his mouth, securing his lips around it. He looked down at the gun resting in his mouth. He could feel the metal irritating the soft palate initiating a gag reflex. His finger slithered around the barrel down towards the trigger. The gagging was becoming more profound by the second. He yanked the gun out of his mouth and thrust it against the counter. The gun spun and fell off the counter with a loud clunk, firing itself on collision; the bullet flew into the fridge door and all this while Rehan threw up intensely all over the kitchen floor.

16th June 2013

Colonel Puri woke up in his large bed on a bright sunny morning, heavy headed and hoarse. He looked down at his wife sleeping peacefully next to him. A smile appeared on his face. He sat on the side of his bed and looked out of the window. An airplane flew across the clear morning sky leaving behind a contrail. The waves swelled gently on the surface of the sea, which reflected the heavens light blue colour.

The Colonel picked up his phone and pressed the voice command button. His voice was weak and tired.

'Call Rehan,' he mumbled.

'Calling Ryan,' his phone announced.

'No! No! Rehan,' he repeated.

'Please identify valid caller,' came the reply.

'REY HAN,' the Colonel said right into the mouthpiece.

'Calling Rehan.'

Colonel Puri let out a frustrated sigh. He seemed nervous about the call and rubbed his eyes while the phone rang a few times.

Rehan lay in bed with his body spread out and a blanket covering him. His head was aching like hell. The massive bout from last night was having its after effects today as he suffered from a nasty hangover. He saw that the Colonel was calling but left his phone ringing. He rolled over and wrapped a pillow around his head.

The call went to voice mail and the Colonel heard Rehan's voice mail message. He sighed in relief.

'Hey Rehan, I was just calling up to check up on you. Well, last night was...fun...no? Actually I wanted to tell you that I have an offer for you. I can get you a job, a proper desk job. Here in my office itself. It will pay a little less, about a lakh a month. Let's just talk about it, okay? Call me.'

Colonel Puri hung up his phone and gingerly placed it on the table. He stared outside for a few seconds before getting up and making his way to the washroom.

❚❚❚

It was a humid afternoon and the city chirruped as people went about their businesses in the peak hours of the day. Rehan drove slowly through the streets with a cigarette in hand resting out his window. He was listening to some reggae on his stereo while rundown Victorian buildings loomed in the background.

Rehan pulled the car into a pay and park and waited for the song to finish. He rested his head back, closed his eyes and nodded to the music. After the song finished he let himself out of the car and treaded the streets of Kala Ghoda.

Sasha was waiting outside the historical Jehangir Art Gallery. As she saw Rehan walk towards her she smiled and waved at him. He waved back at her glumly while moving in towards her dragging his feet.

'Wow, you look like crap,' she said as he walked up to her. 'What's wrong?'

'Don't ask,' he said. 'I had a rough night. Let's walk.'

Rehan and Sasha walked quietly along MG road for a while before she spoke again.

'So where are we going?'

'To Café Coffee Day...I thought,' he said.

She giggled at his response and then continued.

'No, I mean where are we going? After leaving this place... the city. Where should we go? Because I've been thinking...' she paused for a while and Rehan bit his lower lip. His face now wore a sad expression. 'How about somewhere like Bangalore? We could both start working modest...'

Rehan cut her off midway.

'Listen, Sasha. I wanted to talk to you about this later...after coffee. I have some stuff to tell you, regarding the situation.'

'Well, now I'm curious,' she said.

'Can't we just wait...until later?' he asked.

'I won't be able to think of anything else. Just tell me,' she said and waited in anticipation.

Rehan looked at her while processing his sentences in his head.

'Should we at least sit down over there?' he asked pointing at a bench on the footpath.

Sasha nodded and they headed over to the bench. They nestled themselves in and Rehan sighed.

Sasha placed her hand over his and faced him. 'So what's the news?' she inquired.

'Well, I've been thinking. We have nowhere to go,' Rehan began.

'That's the point, we will create a new start,' said Sasha bubbling with enthusiasm.

'How Sasha? Let's face it. You're depressed and I'm probably pretty bummed out. It is not as easy as it sounds.'

'So why do you want to stay?' she asked.

Rehan could see her expressions changing by the second.

'I've been offered a job,' he said. 'It is not a bad one and clean too. But it's here.'

Sasha was now evidently deflated. She rested her face in her hands and shook her head. She let out a muffled scream from under her hands.

'Please, please just listen to me. We'll change here. You and me together. New house and a new start,' Rehan tried to console her.

Sasha brought her face up, her eyes glossy and red. She fought the urge to cry and gave a measly nod. Rehan closed his eyes but there was hurt on his face.

'We'll start fresh. But, we can't just leave,' he said. 'You know that.'

Sasha nodded in understanding.

'We can just leave, it's not rational but it's possible.' She whispered under her breath.

❙ ❙ ❙

The clock on the wall showed 9.55 p.m. Rehan's depressing apartment was in a mess. He hadn't bothered to clean up from last night and the sights along with the smell didn't help his case. Plopped down on the couch; Rehan glanced around the room checking out the ceiling with its water leakages and peeling white paint.

He turned on the TV and zoned out as the blue flashing light from the television lit up his face. The noises of Animal Planet now filled the room. Rehan pulled out a cigarette and lit it. He took a few rips as Animal Planet went into commercial, which made him swear and pick up the remote control surfing through the channels. Rehan stopped on one of those spiritual channels and looked at it with a passive face. A middle aged man with a huge beard and dressed in an orange loincloth with a white shawl was addressing a massive crowd. He emitted an aura of unreal confidence that made Rehan think that perhaps this man knew his shit.

'The biggest mistake that economists make is that they judge the human race, as in fact, rational,' said the man. 'Mankind is not rational. In fact we are the most irrational of all species. I had been in conversation with an Army officer who claimed that a friend of his jumped on an incoming grenade so as to save another officer's life. Who, in the whole animal kingdom sacrifices their own existence for others? Humans, capable of the most infernal and the most divine of actions have been given a choice. A choice we choose to ignore and stumble along the dark passage we think we are in. But once a path is chosen, once we are sure of our choices, we feel enlightened. From a psychopath to a sage, whoever is sure of his actions exudes a certain aura. You can choose yours… '

Rehan dwelled on the man's word for a while. All his life he had taken strong calculated decision for his own well-being. But where had those decisions led him? He had always doubted his actions, questioned his existence. Not anymore…

He walked out onto the balcony and sat in his chair, looking up at the stars. They couldn't be seen clearly due to the light pollution tonight. Mumbai's nightlife was now into its peak hours and people merrily mingled with their friends and loved ones.

Perhaps Sasha was right, he thought. *We could be a little irrational. This place isn't helping anymore. A change of scenery might do us some good.*

Rehan got up and left his seat. He headed right into his bedroom and turned the lights on. He stood at the door motionless for a while. On his desk a picture of Sasha lied facing him. He picked it up and stared at the picture; his hands shook slightly.

'I don't know what to do Sasha. What is the right thing to do?'

Rehan put the picture down and sat on his bed. From under the bed a part of a book stuck out. He grabbed it; *Frost* by Frank. Rehan randomly opened the book and read.

She sits on the rock.
She stares into the sea.
Only to see.
Anything but the sea.

She makes a break.
In order to take,
Over what now seems to be a lake.

Little does she know
That her steps make her go
Towards her final blow.

Insurmountable waves
Dig up graves
For all her misbehaves

But gladly for her
Whose mind was screaming murder!
Peace will be in reach once again.

Rehan looked down at the poem once again and quickly skimmed it over in his head. He sighed and leaned back. Turning to another page he read:

> *Spluttering lights, startled eyes,*
> *Flashes of dark from the eternal bright.*
> *Myriad roads lay entangled,*
> *Where life blinks in surprise,*
> *Until your tottering will and might,*
> *Acceptance has already mangled.*
>
> *Thence all paths do converge,*
> *The only oasis in a desert for miles,*
> *Where every dream does submerge*
> *Until its time again to rise.*
>
> *But what if there's no reprise,*
> *Just a concert in its finale;*
> *The crescendo, you then realize,*
> *Those spurts of colour bright,*
> *A tyranny where darkness reigned,*
> *A revolution only for the trained,*
> *An effort never gone in vain,*
> *At least existence always gained.*
>
> *Doors now shutting against the rain*
> *To nurse a soul so maimed*
> *By the storms that now rage outside*
> *Almost time for a weary demise*
> *In the grave of fireflies.*

Man he was right. This was dark depressing shit. He wondered if it would be advisable to continue reading. After staring at the blank wall for a while he took out his phone and called Sasha.

Sasha sat down on her bed laying down lines of cocaine on the same pink plate. She answered the phone on the fourth ring.

'Hello?' she said dully.

'Sasha...I'm sorry. I really want to make this right,' said Rehan.

'It's already alright. I...I'm just...'

She was lost for words and couldn't explain her feelings. Rehan took the hint and cut her short.

'Well, pack your bags, because we're going to leave,' he said.

'What? Really? When?' she said, each question in increasing loudness and disbelief.

Rehan smiled, closed his eyes and shook his head. Laughing out on her simple adorableness.

'Calm down. I'm serious and the day after tomorrow we're leaving.'

Sasha rested her hands on her forehead and shook her head in happiness.

'And where? Well that's just going to have to be a surprise,' he added.

She looked up at her reflection in the mirror of the dresser as tears slid down her face.

'Okay, that's okay. I like surprises,' she said.

Sasha could hear Rehan's laugh on the other end that made her smile as she wiped the tears with her hand.

Rehan surveyed his room grasping for something else to say. He cleared his throat.

'Well, umm...I'll call you tomorrow with details and a time to meet. We will discuss travel arrangements and all,' he said.

'Yeah, for sure, we'll discuss that tomorrow.'

'Wow, I will just give you time to process... I am yet to digest it too. It's a big move, huh?'

'Rehan,' she said. Her tone was now quieter and sombre. 'I have some money. From my father's, you know, life insurance.'

That was irksome. He didn't say a word lest he say something that might lead down the wrong lane. Finally after a few seconds he opened his mouth to speak but before he could say anything

'So we will talk tomorrow?' she asked.

'Yes, for sure,' he said. 'I love you.'

'I love you too.'

Rehan hung up the phone with a smile on his face. He lay down on the bed and reached out to the Book of Poems. There was happiness in his heart. He knew that he had done the right thing. His smile grew wider and wider the more he thought about it. Finally his misery was coming to an end. And with that feeling of turning over a new leaf he began reading the last poem from the book hoping it might add on to the hopes he had for a decent future.

Power plunges to depths,
That only darkness exceeds.

Light, lending a hand,
To the helpless in the pits.

But to those accustomed to darkness,
Even light appears evil.

While all that is bright,
Illumines the road for all people.

To those born to night,
It exudes a soft glow
While to those born to delight
It lends a bright warm blow.

But all intents are for
This seed not to go to waste.
Because even the smallest mite,
Can sway a mountain in its wake.

So as the yellow waves
Crash on your face,
And tears stream down
Leaving their trace,
Turn your eyes towards the light,
And bathe in the sweet delight
Cause while the fetid also is fecund,
So can you change the nature of your fate.

PART

III

MY NAME IS
REHAN IRANI

EPILOGUE

*M*y name is Rehan Irani and today I am content. I don't say happy because I fear to admit that things are fine lest they take a turn for the worse; call it superstition. Sitting here in my boat in middle of the lake with my friend Gaurav, life seems to have finally given me all what one needs for peace. I take out my saxophone from its case while Gaurav lays out the fishing nets in the water as bright red inflatable mark the spot while we head on to a small rocky cove. This routine has now become a part of my life.

As I start playing a tune, Gaurav listens to me play just like he does every day, lightly tapping the planks of the boat like a bongo. We couldn't make so much noise near the nets lest we scare the fish and the cove lent a cosy feeling; life couldn't be any better than this. The music echoes through these lush green mountains and the birds in them start chirping as if to add in to my melody, creating a beautiful symphony, at least in my mind. I feel like I belong here, in between these mountains and over this bright turquoise lake.

It has been over a year since I left Mumbai with Sasha. I left in search of a better life, happiness, love, inner peace, God and myself. Well I don't know what I have achieved. I definitely haven't found

God; the rest in various degrees comes by and makes it liveable. But I know that away from the din of that city's chocking grid, I am happy and I have found some semblance of that inner peace here in Nainital.

I work as a fish dealer now; which is just a glorified way of saying that I am a fisherman. Gaurav and I are now one of the biggest fresh water fish suppliers in this city. That sounded like a lot but it was a profession of relatively meagre means and lots of free time. I first met him at his father's rundown restaurant some six months back. He used to work as a waiter there. He had this idea of a business but did not have the capital to start it. So I sponsored him, he made me his partner and since then we come here every morning. I am glad I could get him out of that dingy place and help him stand up on his own feet. He was an educated fellow with a keen interest in all things refined, as if his soul yearned for more. We have been great friends since. After Arif, I really needed someone like him in my life to deal with all that it had to offer which was usually a little hard to cope up with.

And yes, that brings me to Sasha. Well I always knew this move was going to be difficult for both of us but for her it was a nightmare. In the early days she was so detached from everything that I almost felt that she regretted doing this every day. Then there were those episodes of mood swings and abdominal cramps, which made me fear the worse. I thought she had some psychiatric condition and that I was going to lose her. She would not talk to me, she would not talk to the doctors, all she would do was sit in her room and cry and cry and cry and not even the cold mountain wind could dry her tears.

But a few months ago things turned around for the better. Finally she showed signs of settling in and I saw glimpses of the old Sasha. I don't know how it happened but I thought that somewhere my love, my patience and my perseverance had paid off. Today she is doing much better and I can see that she too is happy, happy to be with me. I feel her love on an everyday basis now without shadows of self-doubt crossing her face and I think that soon I will ask her to marry me.

As I come to the end of the tune that I am playing, Gaurav applauds with appreciation. I then help him pull the nets out of the water. The catch is good like it usually is considering that there isn't much local competition. Not many people eat fish here and it mainly is distributed domestically and I know we would get a good price for it in the market. We row our boat back to shore and I help Gaurav load the fish in our tempo carrier.

'Will I see you in the evening?' *he asks me.*

'Sure, come over for dinner. Will cook some chicken.' *I tell him.*

'Chicken?' *he winks*

I personally hate eating fish and there were always these jokes on my expense considering my profession.

'Yes, chicken!' *I laugh as he gets into the tempo and drives off towards the market. It is still early in the morning and the humdrum of the town offers no excitement. I decide to head back home and drive my pickup truck to the south of Nainital.*

The wooden cottage where I live is situated a good ten kilometres away from the main market. Its open lawn and spacious rooms are a welcome respite from those cramped up Mumbai apartments.

'Sasha, I am home,' *I announce as I enter the cottage and place my keys on the wood panelled table, slightly rough-hewn but lending a good homely feel to the place.*

There is no response.

'Sasha?' *I call out again.*

Still nothing.

She might be in the washroom, I assume. I make my way to the fridge and pull out a carton of milk. The newspaper is on the dining table and I go through it while eating some cereal from a bowl. I wonder what Sasha is doing. Has she gone back to sleep? I make my way towards the bedroom to check on her.

'Sasha? Sasha!'

She lies on the floor unconscious and motionless. White froth is drooling from the side of her mouth. I rush towards her in a cold sweat and see a thin trail of blood flowing down her nose and onto the floor.

'Sasha! Wake up. Wake up Sasha,' *I shake her but she does not respond. Her breathing is shallow and only through her partly open mouth and her pulse is feeble. I pick her up in my arms and rush out to the car in the blur of panic. After sitting her down in the passenger seat, I recline it a little to ease her breathing and after fastening her seatbelt, I start driving towards the city hospital.*

Oh God, what the fuck happened? I had left her humming over breakfast in the morning, and now this! My mind was reeling over the possibilities and trying to keep the car in the middle of these hairpin bends as it swerved dangerously over the curves. I try to calm myself, breathing deeply and start driving a little slowly, calling out to Sasha intermittently to look for a response, but none comes through the thick veil she is now behind, the pall on her face visible. I reach the hospital ten minutes later and rush her into the emergency room. The doctor on call asks me to wait outside while he rests her body down on the bed. I can see them securing an intravenous line in her arm and resuscitating her as I make my way towards the waiting area.

I call Gaurav to tell him what has happened and he says that he will be here soon. As I sit on a bench in the waiting area I say a soft prayer in my head. I just hope that she is all right and for that I am ready to give up anything. Gaurav arrives a few minutes later and he has some genuine concern in his eyes. I have no explanations to give him for I myself don't know what has conspired.

Some fifteen minutes later the doctor walks out of the ER. He comes up to me and tells me to follow him. We walk down the corridor together and enter his cabin. He goes and sits behind his desk and asks me to take a seat.

'We tried to resuscitate her manually first but that did not help,' *he tells me.* 'Her airways were congested which made intubation difficult. We had to cut open a hole in her neck so that she could breathe again. But as soon as we did that she had a cardiac arrhythmia. We tried our best to stabilize it but her heart stopped working. She did not make it. I am sorry.'

'She...she did not...make it?' *I stammer. His last words were just not sinking in.*

'I am extremely sorry for your loss,' *he tells me.*

The world is drowning out, an anguishing numbness taking over. No, it can't be... Sasha isn't dead. The doctor must be joking; I give him a blank stare as he repeats his condolences.

Argh! The pain, almost physical, can't breathe...Sasha...dead. The love of my life has deserted me. As I tell this to myself the hurt becomes more profound. This could not be happening but it was.

'We suspect that her death was a result of drug overdose,' *the doctor says.* 'Mostly cocaine.'

'Wha...' *I begin and then it strikes me. It is all becoming clear now. That suicidal tendency, those mood swings and psychosis. How did I not see it? She was in fucking withdrawal after moving here and then she became all better. I had been a fool. A knowing yet blind fool who couldn't even arouse enough trust in her so as to learn of her addiction? I could have helped her pull through; the guilt again seeps through my bones, lashing out from within.*

'It is customary to lodge a medico legal case in such cases,' *the doctor tells me.* 'I hope you will co-operate.'

I simply nod as an explosive cocktail of anger and sorrow blends itself inside me.

'Can I see her?' *I ask him.*

'Yes, her body is in the morgue.'

I head out of the doctor's cabin and make my way to the morgue. Her body lies on a bed in a dingy room emitting a stale odour. Rigor Mortis had not set in yet and I clasped her hand in mine, still soft... I sit down on a stool next to her and look at her lifeless face. Suddenly there is no longer any anger but only immense sorrow. Tears come flooding out of my eyes as I hold her hand tightly. I have nothing to say. Nothing can express how I feel right now except maybe if I drown the world in my tears. I have always known that helplessness is the most terrible feeling a man can feel; now I say that from experience.

Someone has sneaked in behind me inside the room. I can sense it.

'Rehan Irani?' *he calls out to me.*

I wipe my tears and turn around. Two men in formal suits stand there looking at me.

'Yes, that is me,' *I tell them.*

'My name is Detective Siddhant Singhal from the Indian intelligence and this is Detective Peter Shawcross from the Interpol,' *he says pointing out at a short, thickset Nordic guy standing next to him, both flashing badges.* 'I am afraid you will have to come with us. You are under arrest.'

I know this has nothing to do with Sasha's death. The Interpol wouldn't be involved. The past had finally caught up with me. Couldn't have been a more beautiful timing... This world had nothing more to offer. I don't even ask them why... just put up my hands as they secure the handcuffs around my wrists. I turn around and look at Sasha one last time before they lead me out of the morgue.

Gaurav walks up to me with a confused expression on his face. Perhaps he deserves some answers. But there is nothing I can give him.

'I will be gone for a while,' *I tell him.* 'Just do me a favour and give her the funeral she deserves. That is all I ask of you.'

He nods solemnly and I know that he will do that for me. The men lead me to their car and help me get into the back seat. The metal of the handcuffs feels cold against my wrist. The car starts moving and with a heavy heart I turn around. I see the city hospital disappearing in the backdrop of this gloomy day. A glorious chapter of my life had come to a tragic end. There are loads of memories to cherish. But then, as some wise old men have said; a new chapter begins where the old one ends and I can't start a new one if I keep re-reading the old ones. But for a while I suppose, the old chapters will be all that give me company. I too know there is more to come but the when and how is shrouded in the mystery called life. Whether it holds pain and suffering or joy and happiness, I don't know.

What I do know is that – My name is Rehan Irani and my story is far from over.